THE LEGACY SERIES

SERIES TITLES

Bodies in Bags
Jamey Gallagher

Apple & Palm
Patricia Henley

A Green Glow on the Horizon
Dawn Burns

How We Do Things Here
Matt Cashion

Neon Steel
Jennifer Maritza McCauley

Release of Information
Kali White VanBaale

The Divide
Evan Morgan Williams

Yes, No, I Don't Know
Kathryn Gahl

The Price of Their Toys
John Loonam

The Caged Man
Calvin Mills

A Day Doesn't Go By When I Don't Have Regrets
J. Malcolm Garcia

These Are My People
Steve Fox

We Should Be Somewhere by Now
Stephen Tuttle

Burner and Other Stories
Katrina Denza

The Plan of Chicago
Barry Pearce

Trust Issues
K.P. Davis

Adult Children
Laurence Klavan

Guardians & Saints
Diane Josefowicz

Western Terminus: Stories and A Novella
Michael Keefe

Like Human
Janet Goldberg

The Hopefuls
Elizabeth Oness

Never Stop Exiting
Michael Hopkins

Broken Heart Syndrome
Anne Colwell

The Mexican Messiah: A Novella & Stories
Jay Kauffmann

Close to a Flame
Colleen Alles

American Animism
Jamey Gallagher

Keeping What's Best Left Kept Secret
David Ricchiute

Soaked
Toby LeBlanc

The Path of Totality
Marie Zhuikov

Shocker in Gloomtown
Dan Libman

The Continental Divide
Bob Johnson

The Three Devils and Other Stories
William Luvaas

The Correct Response
Manfred Gabriel

Welcome Back to the World: A Novella & Stories
Rob Davidson

Greyhound Cowboy and Other Stories
Ken Post

Close Call
Kim Suhr

The Waterman
Gary Schanbacher

Signs of the Imminent Apocalypse and Other Stories
Heidi Bell

What We Might Become
Sara Reish Desmond

The Silver State Stories
Michael Darcher

An Instinct for Movement
Michael Mattes

The Machine We Trust
Tim Conrad

Gridlock
Brett Biebel

Salt Folk
Ryan Habermeyer

The Commission of Inquiry
Patrick Nevins

Maximum Speed
Kevin Clouther

Reach Her in This Light
Jane Curtis

The Spirit in My Shoes
John Michael Cummings

The Effects of Urban Renewal on Mid-Century America and Other Crime Stories
Jeff Esterholm

What Makes You Think You're Supposed to Feel Better
Jody Hobbs Hesler

Fugitive Daydreams
Leah McCormack

Hoist House: A Novella & Stories
Jenny Robertson

Finding the Bones: Stories & A Novella
Nikki Kallio

Self-Defense
Corey Mertes

Where Are Your People From?
James B. De Monte

Sometimes Creek
Steve Fox

The Plagues
Joe Baumann

The Clayfields
Elise Gregory

Kind of Blue
Christopher Chambers

Evangelina Everyday
Dawn Burns

Township
Jamie Lyn Smith

Responsible Adults
Patricia Ann McNair

Great Escapes from Detroit
Joseph O'Malley

Nothing to Lose
Kim Suhr

The Appointed Hour
Susanne Davis

PRAISE FOR
Bodies in Bags

It's best you bring a writing utensil when you crack the spine of Jamey Gallagher's short story collection *Bodies in Bags*. For your writing as well as your own well-being, you're gonna want to steal as much as you can of the dark worldly wisdom Gallagher puts on the page. "The world is rotten and men were cruel," he writes, "and life ended too soon for too many people." To read *Bodies in Bag*s is to bear witness to the steel-hinged, hard-won poetry at work on every page. The best fiction makes us uncomfortable, makes us question if we truly know ourselves and what we might do when pushed to the brink. *Bodies in Bags* is the best kind of fiction. Nobody's safe from addiction within these pages—be it alcohol, drugs, sex, violence, or moral rationalization. There's the art student, the nurse, the teacher, the cop, the drug-dealer, et al. It's your brother, your father, your husband, your boyfriend on the side, all the women stuck in between. I can't imagine him ever doing something like that, you say. To this Gallagher smiles a wry smile, looks off over your shoulder into the middle distance, imagining all the ugliness that you have coming your way down the road. Read your way through *Bodies in Bags* and you'll soon realize that there are no safety blankets, no seatbelts, no social safety nets for the worst that cruel men can reap upon this rotten world.

—BENJAMIN DREVLOW
author of *Honky*

Gallagher's characters and their voices feel so lived in and true—he tackles their stories of navigating complex disturbing situations with writing that is gritty, stark, and honest, and yet shows them grace. His portraits of them are dark, tender, and masterful.

—ANNA VANGALA JONES
author of *Turmeric & Sugar: Stories*

Jamey Gallagher knows his way around the short story form, and in *Bodies in Bags*, his second collection, he serves up slices of hardboiled noir and crime, a mashup of weird-detective fiction, and a touch of postmodernism that Donald Barthelme might have appreciated. This you can bank on: Stephen King said you like it darker; Leonard Cohen said, no, you want it darker. Jamey Gallagher, with *Bodies in Bags*, paints it black.

—JEFF ESTERHOLM
author of *The Effects of Urban Renewal on Mid-Century America and Other Crime Stories*

Bodies in Bags is full of characters both raw and real, who might have been good people in another life. Gallagher makes plots with all the tenderness of a switchblade. Every story is the kind of dark that sheds light on the unwatched corners of life and woven together with words made of lightning and barbed wire. Pages reeking of death come to life to ferret out urges that were just playing possum. And as each character meets the blunt force consequences of their actions, we smash through their humanity like it was a windshield, and are flung far enough to give it all perspective. Gallagher finds the impermanence of living, how close we always are to violence, and then leaves us at the scene of the crime.

—TOBY LeBLANC
author of *Soaked*

BODIES
in BAGS

stories

JAMEY GALLAGHER

CORNERSTONE PRESS
UNIVERSITY OF WISCONSIN-STEVENS POINT

Cornerstone Press, Stevens Point, Wisconsin 54481
Copyright © 2026 Jamey Gallagher
www.uwsp.edu/cornerstone

Printed in the United States of America.

Library of Congress Control Number: 2026930353
ISBN: 978-1-968148-35-5

All rights reserved.

This is a work of fiction. Names, characters, businesses, places, events, and incidents are either the products of the author's imagination or used in a fictitious manner. Any resemblance to actual persons, living or dead, or actual events is purely coincidental.

Cornerstone Press titles are produced in courses and internships offered by the Department of English at the University of Wisconsin–Stevens Point.

DIRECTOR & PUBLISHER
Dr. Ross K. Tangedal

EXECUTIVE EDITORS
Jeff Snowbarger, Freesia McKee

EDITORIAL DIRECTOR
Brett Hill

SENIOR EDITORS
Paige Biever, Ellie Atkinson

PRESS STAFF
Samantha Bjork, Sophie McPherson, Andrew Bryant, Jazymne Johnson, Lilly Kulbeck, Nathan Pearson, Grady Roesken, Asher Schroeder, Sam Zajkowski

This one is for my father, Dan Gallagher.

ALSO BY JAMEY GALLAGHER:

American Animism

S T O R I E S

Charlie's   1

Always and Utter Bullshit   3

A Crash on the Highway   15

Savor Life   25

The Bar Built in an Old Sheet Metal Factory   46

The Feeding   48

Everything Rises   63

Night Moves   66

Butch   80

Idiotic American Boys   85

It Never Snows in Vietnam   102

Redacted Records   113

Artifacts of the Civil War   115

The Resurrection Project   125

San Juan   128

Love as an Act of Revenge   129

The Day after Easter   141

Cam   151

Bodies in Bags   155

The Body in Lake Montebello   158

Dream a Little Dream   170

A Brief but Flaring and Glorious Life   193

Acknowledgments   199

He didn't know if he was capable of pulling anyone back into the light and he didn't know what he was going to do but he knew he was going to have to do something. Ambivalence did not seem to be an option.

—William Gay

Charlie's

A good man yearns for grace, a bad man for redemption. I've never been all that sure which kind I am. I've stood on top of mountains and I've been inside of Charlie's at two p.m. with the rest of the dregs. That girl crossing the street, the bleach blonde who's seen better days? She's taken a piece right out of me. My real life didn't start until after I met her, and then it was forget everything. Home and faith, kith and kin, the old job? I threw it all away and started over. We did all kinds of pills in those days, just threw them all together, pills and booze, to see what happened. But it wasn't a rock star thing. We weren't rock stars. We kept on the edge of everything and fuck all else. This was back when you could live like that near the ocean. We slept on stripped beds, scratchy mattresses, got fleas and bedbugs, but the beach was right there. Got into fights, got arrested. She was worse than me, if you can believe it. This was back before the Mexicans started showing up. Now the Mexicans are always waiting across the street from Charlie's. I don't know who picks them up, but sometimes they're gone. Small household jobs—someone moving furniture, building a shed. I've got no problem with the Mexicans but sometimes they creep me out. All that watching and waiting, what they must be thinking out there, behind those ancient faces with that deep spirituality. Decent people, I'm sure. Me and her, if we get together now we're still popping pills and drinking but it's not like it was before. Maybe because this is the twenty-first century and people like us are out of another era. We're old now. Everyone pushing buttons and reading screens, getting smaller. Those people we used to make fun of, the old vets returned from their world wars, not taking to life so well—those people are us now. Everyone steers clear, plugs in. You can barely talk to anyone anymore.

I've been on top of mountains, but mostly I've been inside of Charlie's, trying to talk to someone. Sometimes I'll walk into the ER at night and just sit there, watching people, mothers and fathers and their sick little kids, some guy with a red towel to his ear, another to his chin, somebody with a nail through his arm. Been waiting so long it don't even hurt, he says, and he's right.

I do odd jobs here and there. I've stood side by side with the Mexicans who don't bother saying one word to me. The beautiful thing about mountaintops is you see the world around you, every little thing except what's hidden beneath the trees. Everything wild. Like the whole world tells you that you're just another dumb animal but lookit here, lookit the world all around. She developed a pretty bad habit—it was those pain pills they gave her after she was run over. They got heavier prescriptions now. She'll pop those and swill some beer and then just lie wherever, with whoever, not caring about a damn thing. C'mon baby, get on up, let's go to Charlie's, I'll say, and she'll look at me like she can't see nothing, or like I am nothing. Redemption, I guess. That's what I'm looking for. Grace seems a little too much to ask at this point.

Always and Utter Bullshit

1

It was barely morning when I walked out of the woods onto the road, but it felt like I'd been walking for-fucking-ever. My legs were tired and I was cold. The sun was somewhere behind the mountains, giving everything that weird in-between feeling, like right before something happens. I didn't know what was going to happen, probably nothing more than the sun coming up over the mountains, but it felt like *something* was going to. One thing that was definitely going to happen was Erikson was going to follow me. He was not going to just let me leave. Not that I was all that worried.

When I came out onto the road, I took the bills from my pocket and fanned them out in my hand, the way I'd been doing over and over again since we'd left Massapequa, when he'd handed me the roll to hold, trying to impress me. I couldn't believe he didn't realize I still had the money. Seven hundred dollars altogether. Coming out onto the road I realized how stupid it was to carry the money around that way, so I put the roll into this slit in my jacket, a secret compartment. The jacket was leather and not as warm as it should have been, so my hands were pink from the cold.

I looked up and down the road, trying to get a sense for which way to go, though either way was as good as the other. I turned right and went that way. The ice crunched beneath my shoes and I tried not to think about the fact that I'd fucked Erikson the night before, let him fuck me, rather, that—who knows—there was a possibility that he'd impregnated me, which was just what I fucking needed, right. I didn't care about the sex, I was long past the stage where I thought sex could mean something, and in the long run it still gave me the upper hand, but I should have insisted on a condom at least.

After driving me up to his cabin, Erikson'd been sick for a few days and now he wasn't sick but wasn't back to who he'd been before, which was someone who liked to be in control. It was hard to remember why I'd agreed to come up here with him. There was the whole illicit nature of the thing that got me going. I knew I shouldn't have been doing it, so that's why I did it. I'd met him at a student art exhibit at the college. He'd come up to me and told me he liked my painting, a portrait of a man who'd just been bashed over the head with an ax. I'd looked at a ton of Google images to get the look of the brains just right. It wasn't easy. Most of my peers thought the painting was crap, nothing but shock value, but there was a deeper quality to it. It was an act of retribution, sure, because the face looked a little like my brother, a little like my father, but it was more than that, too. And it was *good*. This older guy in his stupid gray suit, a teacher at the art school I'd never had, recognized that. Erikson. I looked into his eyes. There was something in there, some real deep darkness. I mean, he was obviously coming on to me, doing that whole lecherous middle-aged guy thing, but there was something else at work, too.

When I decided to drop out of Massapequa, it was Erikson I went to tell. He closed his office door and sat me down. "Now why do you want to drop out, again?" he said, and I spilled it: how pointless the whole fucking enterprise was. I told him I'd been shooting up for a few months and was probably addicted, and he nodded and told me he could help. "I can help you get clean," he said. "I have a place up in the mountains. One weekend is all it would take." I knew he wanted to get me alone so he could fuck me, but the offer was also sincere. He really wanted to get me clean. I wound up bawling and he held me against his chest, and even though I was right there he didn't try anything. "There, there," he said. He actually said that. It was weird because we were both there in the moment, these reactions and emotions were real, but we were also acting them.

"Can I take you away for the weekend?" he said. "Let me. Please?"

I nodded. He told me he'd pick me up outside my dorm, and I didn't believe he would, but there he was in the morning.

I kept touching the roll of bills through my coat. It was like when you have a sliver of skin on the edge of your fingernail and you keep working at it until you peel it off.

The sun crawled over the mountains and it got warmer. I was wondering what would happen if a car didn't come by and pick me up soon, whether there was a possibility Erikson would catch up to me and what he would do to me if he did. I didn't think he would hurt me or tie me up or kill me or anything, but he would definitely do *something*. He would have to. A truck passed, crunching tires over ice starting to slush up, the driver ignoring my outstretched thumb. I tried to look like someone's daughter. I was no one's daughter anymore. Sometimes I didn't even think of myself as a person anymore, because if you think of yourself as a person you have to start acting like one. I didn't think of myself as a machine or an alien or anything like that, but I thought of myself as just a mammal, with all the normal mammalian drives, for sustenance and warmth, shit like that. A mammal with mammal eyes that looked at the world trying to figure out what it needed to do to survive.

Finally another pickup appeared. This truck pulled onto the side of the road, its tires compressing the snow, making a sound that made my head ache, and the driver reached over and flung open the door. He was youngish, with a neck beard and dark eyes under a thick brow ridge. "You've got a nice face," I told him when I climbed in.

"Uhn, where you heading?"

"I have no idea." I could almost hear his thoughts ratcheting around in his dumb he-brain.

"Do you party?" he asked. "You want to get high?"

"Do I?" I smiled at him then turned away. I could see my reflection in the side mirror—it looked like I didn't have any eyebrows or eyelashes.

2

No way was I going to tell Heath, the guy in the truck, I had a roll of seven hundred dollars hidden in my jacket. I told him I was broke and had no place to crash and he told me not to worry because he lived in a house with a bunch of "buddies" and nobody cared who crashed there. Maybe I could clean the dishes once in a while. Whatever. He drove me a ways away, close to this town with a state college nearby, not far from a ski lodge, to this big dark wooden house at the bottom of a mountain. Red Solo cups, beer cans, and pizza boxes in heaps on the slushy porch. We walked right into a scene like a million other scenes I'd walked in on before, wastoids lounging on couches with a video game on a flatscreen TV and some weird-ass music playing everywhere. They were potheads, which was deeply disappointing.

When I stepped into the room they perked up, thinking they were going to get something off me, which was not going to happen, not at all if I could help it and as a last resort if I couldn't. They were a mix of college guys and a few locals. Heath was one of the locals who also went to the college. He scratched his neck and looked at me and took some bong hits, and I could feel him falling in love with me already, which was fine with me because that would keep the others off me. I had to figure out a way to leverage this. They told me to take off my jacket, get comfortable, but I told them I didn't want to just yet, that all I wanted was to score some meth. When they realized I wasn't joking they called someone. The place smelled of pot smoke, spilled beer, old pizza. They were probably looking for a mother. Just what I needed.

It was difficult to hear or concentrate on anything with the music blaring from another room and the sound of a video game like a cataclysm of metal rending, gunshots, and explosions. They'd surrounded themselves with noise to push away their fear of death—or life. I washed my face and thought maybe I wouldn't actually do the crystal once it showed up, maybe I'd just keep it in reserve, though my body was already priming for it, dilating like an eye, opening like a mouth. It wasn't like I was addicted to meth—I'd done it a handful of times—but the heroin jones was gone and I was ready for a new high, something else to let myself down inside of. I'd been straight for three days, total, up there in the mountains taking care of Erikson, and seen the world through regular, if withdrawn, eyes, and it was nothing I wanted to do much more of if I could help it. I sat on the toilet. Piss coated the floor, pubes were piled in the corners, smears of toothpaste and dried shaving cream flecked the sink. It was gross, but I didn't want to leave and go back to Massapequa, which I couldn't do anyway, or back to my so-called family, which no thanks, and Erikson was out of the question since I had absconded with his seven hundred dollars.

When we'd been driving up from Massapequa, he'd thrown the roll into my lap and said, "We'll have some fun," kind of ironically but not. He'd told me he wanted to get me clean—playing the caring father—but then he threw the money in my lap and I knew the weekend was going to be different from what I'd expected, which was okay with me. As soon as we got to the little cabin in the mountains, though, he fell asleep. In the middle of the night, he started puking. I had to help him to the outhouse, where I could hear him having the shits, and I had to start all the fires and cook all the meals, while I was fucking withdrawing, swearing and shaking and all that shit, but pretty mildly since I hadn't been a junkie long. All I wanted to do now was be alone and get high.

I could hear other people in the house now, whoever was bringing the meth, and I peeled off a couple hundreds from the roll, crumpled them in my fist, shoved them in my jeans pocket. I came out and paid for an 8 ball—the dealers were scumbags who differed from the college guys, only in the fact that they were older and had given up all hopes of gainful employment—which I smoked in a little pipe Heath gave me. He watched me with big sad eyes, scratching his neck now and then, not asking how I came up with the money when I'd said I was broke.

After ten minutes I was high and taking his keys and going out to his truck and doing donuts in the driveway before racing down to town. He looked scared because he *was* scared. I didn't give a shit. In town there were a few people around and I honked the horn, which actually no shit played the rebel call or whatever it's called. I was just *flying*, feeling good, driving up and down the mountains, tearing shit out of the world. Heath and me were on totally different trips. He was on pot and spaced out while I just wanted to *do* something even though there was nothing to do up here.

The night before I escaped from the cabin, I drank a lot out of this bottle of old whiskey Erikson had in the cabinet and I slept with him for the first and last time. It was one of those lazy fucks where you pretend nothing is happening. He was still a little sick and I could feel his body heat, and I was drunk, and these things happen. I was jonesing, but not hard. The alcohol helped. My body was hungry for disorientation and it would take whatever it could get. In the morning I was hungover, but I realized I had to get away from this guy, because he was toxic and weird and now that he'd known physical intimacy it was bound to lead to real problems.

Somehow I ended up spinning Heath's truck into a snowbank. I remember the moment the tires lost traction, how perfect it felt, exactly everything I had ever wanted in the world because I was no longer there at all. Just spinning.

3

It's like diving into a wave pool is what the life of a meth user is like, negotiating all these waves. Sometimes you're up and sometimes you're down, and you're riding it and you know your life is completely fucked, but you don't care. You become this other thing. You throw away whatever you used to be, or it curls up tight and tiny like one of those pill bugs and sinks deep inside you, and all you care about is maintaining this high. Sometimes you feel this weird anger race through you. I must have punched Heath in the face three times, and I was always wrestling him, throwing him down on the floor, which made his buddies laugh, though they didn't fuck with me because they knew they couldn't take me. Sometimes the guys looked at me out of the corners of their eyes like they were scared of me, like I was something out of another world they had never intended to enter. I shaved off the ice with a razor blade and smoked it throughout the day, and when that 8 ball was gone I made Heath invite the guys over again so I could buy another 8 ball. I felt like the money would last forever, which of course it never does, does it? It can't, because that's the nature of money. To disappear.

Sometimes Heath would be gone during the day and I'd sit alone in the living room, feeling lucky. I am someone who can spend all her time alone. The best times I had with my last boyfriend were when he'd leave me alone for days and I could shoot up and just veg in front of the TV. I go through intense productive artistic phases when I don't want to see anyone—that's when I painted my series of ax-murder portraits. This meth thing was a whole different animal, though, all highs and lows. Sometimes I had to get out, so I walked around the little town, which had this white steeple church and people who actually no-shit chopped their own wood and wore flannel shirts and jeans. It was too much. The college kids all got drunk on weekends like they were following a script. I felt safe here.

The deal with Heath was that he was shy and had completely fallen in love with me. The schmuck. His neck beard didn't grow any thicker and he never seemed to shave it off. He looked the same all the time. He didn't have any fashion sense, he wasn't funny, and he sure as hell wasn't good looking. He was a million other guys just taking up space. I didn't really like him, but I didn't hate him. I was just relieved he was there so the others stayed away from me, which they did, even though sometimes I could sense this vibe coming off them, like, let's slip her something. Or, how long is this chick going to stay here? I figured when that question came up was when I'd have to start putting out. I hoped putting out to Heath would be enough. They lived this sad little life where they thought they were cool because they were fucked up all the time and they didn't do any schoolwork.

When I crashed I writhed on the floor of the living room, wishing I was dead, and Heath would put a blanket over me. He was sweet but so fucking dumb. I never heard him say anything that could be considered even relatively intelligent. It was like he didn't *think*. I made him take me out every couple days. Sometimes I drove like a crazy person and sometimes he drove, and I would tune the radio to some pop crap and sing loud. I could tell he was trying to figure out how to make his move. I found this ski mask on the floor one day and made him drive me to the local Esso where I pretended to have a gun in my coat and the woman, this old lady with black hair and pockmarks all over her face, handed over $107, which was disappointing but kept me going. Heath was shitting bricks, but the poor boy had no choice. He'd do whatever I wanted him to. He just about creamed his pants when I leaned over and kissed him on the cheek. I had this bottled-up feeling and I knew that this thing, living in Heath's house and getting tweaked, wasn't going to last much longer. I was bored with it. I had no clue how many days or weeks had passed, but I noticed that winter was either over or just about. After I bought another 8 ball I was out of money and I smoked it and smashed some stuff in the kitchen—plates, mostly. Maybe I'm a little nuts, I don't know, but it helped. The boys didn't like it too much, though, and they had a heart-to-heart with Heath and you know what that means.

4

Heath drove like a little old lady, hunched behind the wheel, so fucking slow, careful because he was high which was fine, a long, boring ride. He was suddenly on this country music kick, so I had to listen to someone singing about beer and trucks and broken hearts. I wanted to scream sometimes, but I was determined to be nice to him, at least for now. All I wanted to do was smoke some meth. Barring that I wanted to rip the skin off my skeleton, strip it all away. I pictured my eyeballs dangling out of my skinless face. This thing of meat. They were bad thoughts, so I watched the woods on either side of the road and tried not to think them. I bit at the corner of my thumb, where the little ridge of meat rises up around the thumbnail, and picked at this pimple that had been on my face for weeks. I gouged away. Heath tried to talk once in a while, like "where are we going," but I didn't say anything and he couldn't keep a conversation going to save his life. He was dropping out of college, moving away from the only world he'd ever known, for me, which was fucking hilarious.

As we got closer to the city, he hunched even further over the wheel. He was so scared of the city I could hear his heart jackrabbiting in his chest. And then, there we were in the city and he was driving around all panicked saying "where we going, where we going," while yellow taxis zipped around us, almost clipping our bumper. It was like a circular tank at an aquarium, all these sharks zipping around, all pushing each other on, and if one of them stops the whole thing's going to go to hell so nobody stops. It was a nice day, the sun shining off the sides of taxis, and I felt high even though I wasn't which was almost but wasn't enough to make me feel a little better. "Where the fuck are we going?" Heath almost yelled. I pointed him down streets and we wound up driving past the heart of the city, then farther south. If we went far enough we'd get into an entirely different part of the city and then out of the city altogether into ethnic enclaves and shit. Places we didn't want to go, where we would not be welcome.

I didn't think I knew where we were going but pretty soon we were in a neighborhood of brownstones that was familiar, and there it was, like a sign, an omen: an empty parking space. Heath almost hyperventilated trying to parallel park. By the time he shut the engine off his hand was quivering and his breath was coming in grunts and it wouldn't have surprised me if he started crying. "Where the fuck are we? I'm going back. I'll drop you off and just go back. I have to go back." His eyes bugged out of his head. I waited a few minutes for him to calm down, then placed my hand on his denim-jacketed arm and looked deep into his eyes, kind of gathering him to me with whatever internal power I might have.

"Listen," I said. "You're not going anywhere. Man up, dude. You're with me. Everything's going to be fine." Which was bullshit. Always and utter bullshit. Nothing was ever fine. But you could find a way to ride it out. I had no idea what I was going to do, and as I walked up to the brownstone I realized I'd never been here alone, but it didn't matter because the dude didn't seem surprised when he opened the door. He had silver hair and wore a suit with a sheen, kind of sophisticated. "Oh," he said. I didn't know how he could have recognized me because I'd been here only once with an ex-boyfriend when I lived in the city, before Massapequa, and my hair was a different color then. But it was pretty obvious why we were there.

He let us into the apartment, big and open, kind of modern, like he shopped at a high-end Ikea. Ikea for rich folks. He was listening to some kind of weird jazz. "Sit down," the man said, so we did. He was drinking a glass of wine and exuding this whole sense of New York City and danger and sophistication, and I wondered what the hell he was doing alone dressed like that, then figured he was probably going out later because it was still early, for the city. He looked at Heath, then ignored Heath and looked at me. "You're looking for something," he said.

"What do you have?"

"What do you want?"

"Heroin?"

He smiled one of those smiles, amused and superior. He was the kind of guy who would kill someone violently but quietly. He took out a wooden box from under the couch and took out his works and we cooked up and tied off and shot up right there, the needle sinking into my arm almost sensuously, like a dance, and then I was off. He was a beautiful man, and high his eyes sagged, his lantern jaw unhinging.

Heath sat in a corner of the room watching like some horrified golem. The future was about as clear as milk. Something might have been stirring to life inside me, but I had no way to know it at that moment. I wanted to paint Heath—his face a series of colors you would never expect his face to be—but wasn't sure I would ever paint again.

A Crash on the Highway

Javi and Trent had been driving eighteen hours straight when they ran into two lanes of stopped traffic on I-84 in northern Utah. Eight a.m., the sun was already unremitting, turning the scruffy hills on both sides of the black highway yellow, even the creosote bush. The new tar on the interstate threw heat waves, and through those waves Javi stared at a series of brake lights arrayed in front of him. After ten minutes, drivers started turning off their engines, emerging from their vehicles to stand in the sun. They were almost all white, sunburned, wearing sleeveless t-shirts, cargo shorts, and sandals. The women wore blouses with loose collars. Normal, everyday people.

"What the fuck," Javi said, though he didn't feel any way about the jam at first.

"I'll bet it's a crash," Trent said.

"No shit it's a crash."

Javi slid out of the 80's model Mustang they'd stolen in Boise to stretch in the sun. The temperature would top a hundred again, easy, but was in the 80s now. Javi was built like a flyweight, compact and lithe, his dark red skinny jeans sagging in the back, his gray tank top loose. Reaching around, he rubbed the tat he'd been given in High Desert State Prison, a Satanic symbol on the nape of his neck, scratched out in blue ink. He hadn't struggled when they gave him the tattoo, knowing that struggling wouldn't stop anything and would just make the tat come out shitty, but the tat had come out shitty anyway. Most people couldn't tell what it was. Which was all to the good.

Shoving his hands deep in his pockets, Javi shuffled along the side of the highway, the one-foot strip of breakdown lane. Some of the people who'd stepped out of their cars glanced at him, maybe sensing that he was not of their world, that he only surfaced in their world at gas stations or bars, best to be avoided, but most ignored him. He could have been anyone to them, so he was no one.

Dust caught in his eyes, turning the corners of his vision soft, but when he blinked the dust away everything came into sharp focus again, the world too damn clear. A few cars ahead, a trailer full of pigs rattled inside their enclosures, every few minutes a sound like something struggling against its bindings. Javi could see just an ear or a pink teat through the holes in the metal grates. The truck driver sat impassively, mustached face shaded under a baseball cap, watching as Javi walked past.

As he drew closer to the crash site, the crowds clotted up, standing in the dusty median. White folks with red faces. A skinny redheaded kid wearing a red t-shirt. Tractor trailers and cars sped past going the other direction on I-84 with a sound like the universe tearing in two then sewing itself back up again quick.

Finally, after walking about a half mile, he was at the crash site itself. A bright red pickup truck mashed and mangled against the back of a tractor trailer. The metal looked seared and scarred, as if it were as sensate as skin. The state police had arrived already but no tow truck. A helicopter hovered, preparing to land, raising dust clouds that reached the edge of the crowd, and Javi realized he must have been hearing it for a while without recognizing the sound or letting it touch him. The cops had opened what remained of the driver's side door and were struggling to drag a limp body out, a big guy wearing a ball cap, his t-shirt pulled up to expose a fish-white belly. The face was bleeding, the left side of the body as crumpled as the pickup.

Javi had seen plenty of dead bodies in his life, beginning with his brother Luis, beaten to death by their father when they were kids, in Nevada. The bastard had disappeared after that. He probably hadn't intended to kill anyone. Their father was a square jaw, a squat body, nothing more. Javi couldn't even remember the old man's voice. He remembered how heavy Luis had been, how he had not been Luis at all, just this empty weight, this suit that kind of still looked like Luis. The man in the truck was not dead yet, but his hold on life was tenuous. EMTs from the heli strapped him onto a body board before loading him in, then the helicopter took off in a wide arc.

It would be a while before the truck and debris, a long shit-trail of chrome parts from the pickup, were cleared from the road, but Javi turned and walked back past the same people, who were familiar to him now the way people on a TV show were. Trent sat waiting in the Mustang, staring straight ahead.

"Yo, what happened? Someone die?"

"Nah, bro. It's all cool."

Trent nodded. When another cop car passed, half on the road, half in the desert, lights flashing, Trent flinched.

"Are they going to be there still, if we show up late?" Javi said.

Trent shrugged. "Maybe, yeah. I think."

Souls were supposed to rise. That was the whole idea of souls. They were supposed to take flight once a person "passed," but instead Javi felt the pickup truck driver's soul fall out of the helicopter. It freefell down through the crystalline air before slamming against the hot dry ground, so hard it raised a cloud of yellow dust. The guy had most likely led a straight life—had a wife, probably, kids, a nine-to-five. He'd tried to do some good in this world. Had struggled and strived like anyone else. Javi saw his soul sitting there in the desert like a black box that could never be opened again and felt envious.

He popped three more pills from a plastic baggie in the glove box and rocked forward. It would be another hour before they were able to drive again, speeding across the high desert, but he was fucking ready.

By the time they were allowed through, the crash had been cleared and the red truck rested by the side of the road, crushed beyond reckoning, reminding Javi of the body of some prehistoric animal dredged out of the ground. Some kind of beast. He felt a little sorry for the truck, which would no doubt be crushed now, turned into something else.

Hours of zoned out driving on I-84, traveling deeper into Utah, 83-85 miles per hour, passing trucks on the left while giving everyone a wide berth because no way he was going to end up like the putz in the red pickup. Javi also wasn't going to drive like an asshole and get pulled over, risking everything. They didn't see a single cruiser on the road all morning. He pulled off the interstate where Trent told him to, an exit with no services.

He'd been "working" with Trent for two years now, ever since his release. They'd been in school together, back in the day. They had never been friendly, but Javi had sold Trent weed, and after he was sent away Trent moved in to fill the void. They went in together on a few jobs. Javi didn't like or trust Trent—didn't understand why he didn't appreciate the family he had, a mother, a father, both with decent jobs, a nice rancher—but acted like they were best friends, because of this, because of where they were going right now. Trent had hooked it all up. Nobody involved even knew Javi's name.

Trent pushed in the CD that had been in the car when they stole it, and for the fifth time they listened to the heavy metal album, a band called Pantera Javi had never heard of, not that he had much time for music. This music was thick, turgid, full of thrashing guitars that reminded Javi of the time he'd gone down the Colorado River on an inflatable raft. They weren't supposed to be there, were in a restricted area, but who the fuck was going to stop them. He'd wound up face down in the water, the sound of the rapids filling his head. The heavy metal was like that.

Trent pointed him left and right and right again until they came to a little town on the edge of the desert with nothing in it but an old closed motel, its broken windows letting in the sand when the wind blew, and an old gas station that was also closed. The gas station's old-fashioned oval sign was sandblasted to hell, impossible to read, the pumps like something out of a black-and-white movie. Trailer homes were scattered around, like no one had thought about the footprint of the town. They passed a trailer where a woman watered a dead lawn, the water looping out in sad arcs from the end of the hose. Trent pointed to an old brick building that looked like it had been there since pioneer times, one of the few places with a patch of green lawn, and Javi pulled in.

Surprisingly, it was a house, a normal everyday house that looked like it had been lifted out of someplace much nicer, Moab or something. When Javi grabbed his .44 out of the glovebox, Trent looked at him but didn't say anything. What was he going to say? Javi saw it again: the soul of the pickup driver falling out of the helicopter and thudding onto the desert floor. He thought of his brother Luis, who he hadn't thought about for years, and his father, who he hadn't stopped thinking about for years. He thought about the guy who had marked him with the tattoo in High Desert, initiating him into something he had no desire to belong to. He secured the .44 against the small of his back and arranged the tank top over it, while Trent went around to the back of the Mustang to grab the backpack. The car smelled like burning oil, the metal of its hood clicking as it cooled. Hard to believe anything could cool here. It was more than a hundred degrees. The motion of the road kept moving behind Javi's eyes and he was thirsty as fuck.

At the front door of the house waited a man and a woman, both late middle-aged, the man at least a foot taller than Javi. He didn't wear a cowboy hat but looked like he should have been. His face was dark, the skin thin, as if Javi could see straight through to his skull. He wore a thick mustache like Wyatt Earp but was all business. The woman, small, looked like a grandmother in a storybook, roly poly, wearing a white shirt with an American flag embroidered on it, denim shorts that looked like a skirt. Her legs were covered in cellulite it was hard not to notice. Javi nodded, smiled, acting harmless, and let Trent do all the talking.

They sat in an air-conditioned living room with matching furniture and a deep forest green carpet that brushed against the sides of Javi's sandaled feet. The place made him feel dirtier than before. It didn't smell like anything. The woman offered them sweet tea, but Javi asked for a glass of ice water instead, which he drank so fast it gave him a headache. Trent and the couple talked like distant relatives, telling each other how they'd been, mentioning names Javi didn't recognize. At one point the old man took the backpack and walked out of the room, and when he returned, he replaced it by Trent's feet. They said their goodbyes. Javi was reluctant to leave the cool house. He looked around as if he could hold it with him.

As Javi drove away, Trent lifted out glassine packages of meth from the body of the backpack. Hundreds of them, prettily packaged. He took out a small packet, cut some up, using a math textbook that had been in the back of the Mustang and a maxed-out credit card, and snorted it from the crux of his thumb and his pointer finger, then cut more for Javi.

"The big score," Trent said. "The big fucking score!" He pounded the dashboard and laughed, and Javi just looked at him.

The full flush of the high was immediate, sending him speeding down the long empty desert roads. Now the heavy metal sounded new and hard and perfect, a thing newborn into this world. The high was better and more intense than sex, which might be why Javi hadn't had sex in almost a year and didn't really miss it. He kept his usage reasonable, was not hooked on crank, not really, though he did feel shitty if he didn't get at least one bump a day. He wasn't ever going to be like some meth-heads he saw, losing their teeth, demeaning themselves to get cash to score. He could maintain. Though probably not forever. He would have to push forward into real use or leave the shit behind forever. Eventually.

Trent had him pull over so he could take a piss, and Javi got out of the car to stretch. The endless desert. It felt like getting out of the cockpit of a jet or after a long journey across space. He couldn't remember the last time he had paused. 112 degrees, the day was hot and dry, and the second he stepped into it he felt thirsty again. He got out the emergency gallon jug of water from the back and drank. The water was lukewarm but glugged around the sides of his mouth and refreshed him.

While Trent was still pissing, Javi took out the .44, walked over and pressed the barrel against the back of Trent's head. He saw a scab through the fuzz of Trent's short hair. He was just a white boy trying hard to disappoint his family. Trent dribble-pissed to nothing and stood, his dick out, waiting. Javi let seven seconds pass before pulling the trigger, a loud sudden shot that sent his arm recoiling and reverberated until the sound was swallowed by the desert. Trent's brains raveled out about three feet in front of him, but it was less messy than Javi had expected. He imagined picking up the brains and shoving them back into the skull, imagined Trent getting up and holding the hole in his head, laughing about it. "What the fuck did you do that for, bro?"

Javi shrugged, walked back to the Mustang, drove away, the backpack open on the passenger seat beside him. He filled up at a travel center before leaving the main highway again for a county road through the desert. Dozens of people were crowded into the travel center, at least fifteen lined up at the Subway counter waiting to buy food that didn't taste like real food. An old man with little braids in his long white hair, wearing a full get-up, leather chaps and a buckskin shirt, an old white man who wished he was an Indian, was last in line. Javi couldn't remember the last time he'd eaten. He wasn't hungry but bought a plastic package of salted peanuts anyway, and another gallon of water, and he downed some handfuls of peanuts, washing them back with the last of the lukewarm water.

He sped down County Road 6, passing trucks, weaving in and out of traffic, stopping sometimes to take a snort. He didn't want to get too fucked up but wanted to maintain his buzz. He pulled off and cut up five packages into powder, placed the powder in an old film container he'd had for years, drove on.

Night fell as if it didn't want to, bands of peach and light blue layering themselves on the horizon for what felt like hours. The first star appeared in the east, in a dark blue, almost purple quadrant of the sky. It was pretty, Javi guessed, though it had a bad energy that made him think of the tat on the back of his neck and what the people who put it there would do on a night like this. When the engine light lit up on the dashboard, he ignored it, pushing the Mustang harder. He was past the ability to think about safety or the future. He pushed the car up to 110 miles per hour over a pass in the desert where he saw eyes reflecting like pennies in the night.

The Mustang gasped, then a loud knock sounded from inside the engine compartment, like something huge and angry trying to get out. The car sputtered to a halt. Javi pulled it off the road then took out the lug wrench from the well in the trunk and smashed the windows with it. It took more effort than he expected but felt real good. He stood on the hood kicking in the remainder of the windshield with his sandals. It reminded him of a picture he'd seen of a man in a riot smashing a cop car. He felt clean and pure and entirely alone as he grabbed the backpack and the fresh gallon of water and walked into the desert.

Now that night had taken hold, it settled in. Stars multiplied. He could feel the day's heat radiating off the sand as he headed toward some rock structures in the distance that looked like a dark, silent city.

After his father had beaten Luis to death and abandoned them, Javi had vowed to kill the man, to hunt him down and make him pay, no matter how long it took. He had imagined elaborate means of revenge, pulling the fucker's toenails out, stringing him up on a tree, not so he died from a broken neck but so he suffocated, a long, slow, painful death. In addition to Luis, their father had also beaten their mother, who'd drank too much and fucked around with too many men in town. Javi had loved her and been ashamed of her at the same time. When he was sixteen, he'd ventured out to find his father, traveled all over Nevada, Utah, Idaho, Colorado, but the man was nowhere to be found. Dead or hidden so well no one would ever find him. He'd talked to men in bars, men at the edge of the world, showed them photographs. There were a lot of shaking heads.

When he reached the stone formations, Javi took out the film container, snorted more than he usually would. He just kept snorting. It was dark now and the heat had almost entirely left the earth. Before long it would be cold. Hard to believe. He had no idea what kinds of animals lived out in the desert at night. Wild cats, maybe. He wasn't afraid of anything. Slinging the backpack over his shoulder and feeling for hand- and footholds, he climbed the stone formation, which was basically a little mountain range in the middle of the desert, like the landscape of hell. The moon was half-full, and he could see clearly by its light.

As he climbed he realized that he'd left the .44 back in the Mustang, that if he was going to kill himself out here he was going to have to do it some different way, maybe with his pocketknife. He wished more than anything that he could take his soul out, that it was lodged inside a box in his chest or just behind the tat on the back of his neck and he could figure out some simple way to dislodge it. If he could, he would leave it right there in the middle of the fucking desert and walk away from it.

Savor Life

The sidewalk was still stained where the insured had landed, reddish-brown Rorschach blots against gray concrete. Resisting interpretation, Reyersen slid black-and-white photos out of a Manila folder and held them away from his face, telescoping his arm because he was nearsighted. One of the stains on the sidewalk was from the crick of blood that had leaked out of the man's mouth, another from the brains that had escaped the cage of his skull when it cracked open against concrete. The poor sap. Or the fortunate fellow. If what he'd intended was to end his life, he had ended it, definitively, in one violent stroke. In the photo the man wore a tan raincoat over a black suit. His tie hung loose around his neck, exposing the hairy notch below his Adam's apple. He'd landed on his back. Reyersen imagined him waving his arms and legs as he fell, as if he could catch on to something in the air and hold himself back.

The man had worn glasses. The wire frame had come loose from around one of his ears. The close-up photos of the man's head had an artistic look, like they'd been shot by Man Ray. Disquieting, but also aesthetically appealing. Reyersen wondered how drastically the features had been jarred out of shape, how different the man would have looked before his head impacted the pavement. The face in the photo looked lopsided, but also dependable, the kind of guy you could trust. There were dozens of men like that at Savor Life, the insurance company Reyersen worked for. The logo of the company was a white bird against a blue circle, a positive spin on the insurance business. Everything public-facing about the company exuded positivity. Reyersen worked the dirty jobs. Jobs like this, where he had to determine whether someone had killed himself, been killed, or whether the fall had been, as reported, an "accident."

He compared the photos to the sidewalk again before sliding them back into the folder and crouching. He touched the rough concrete, then lay in the position Ed Wholley had been in when he landed. The sidewalk was on a side street, an alley, really, so there wasn't a lot of foot traffic, but a young couple walked past arm-in-arm, cutting through to get to the next street, glancing down at him curiously. Not that Reyersen cared. He had a job to do, and he was damn-well going to do it.

On this cool early March day, birds had returned to the city. A few crows hunched on the molding of the building across the alley, a brownstone that'd been there forever. The building from which Wholley had fallen, on the other hand, was modern, built within the last ten years—new but far from nice, a brutalist structure that already looked in need of repair, if not demolition. A cheap hotel with small balconies attached to the sides of all the rooms, it didn't jibe with the older buildings in the area, with their cornices and brick faces. It looked temporary. Glancing up at the top of the building gave Reyersen vertigo.

He placed his cheek against the stained concrete, which smelled like ozone and iron, then looked up at the sky between the buildings. The "accident" had occurred eight days earlier, on one of those gray February days that feel both interminable and too short, days that shut down like guillotine blades, days everyone was happy to see end. Reyersen raised his arms and legs in the air, shook them a little.

A man wearing a raincoat identical to the one Wholley had worn passed on the sidewalk, his face hidden.

Reyersen clambered up from the pavement, brushing grit off his jacket. It was a little after lunch—he'd downed a crab cake at a local bar with two colleagues—and he felt full and, thanks to the martinis, logy, yet the case intrigued him. Not because there was any great mystery to it but because he recognized something of himself in Ed Wholley, the part he wanted to kill off.

He entered the hotel from the side door in the alley, a simple red door with no windows or markings of any kind, unlocked. The maroon carpeting inside was thin, the walls dark, half the lightbulbs in their cages on the wall dead. The ammoniac stench of urine rose from one corner. A large man, as hairy and stout as a wrestler, emerged from a room down the hall, clad in an undershirt and loose gray pants. A towel, even from this distance visibly dotted with blood and snot, was draped over his shoulder, and he held a shaving mug and razor. He passed Reyersen with a grunt, possibly of warning. A little down the hallway, Reyersen heard the sounds of what might have been sex or might have been a physical altercation behind one of the doors. He had his money on sex but wasn't going to hang around to collect.

He eschewed the elevator and climbed the stairs to the tenth floor, the floor Wholley had "fallen" from. The stairwell was dark, his footsteps echoing against concrete. A lightbulb flickered on one of the landings. He had the feeling only prostitutes and drunks ever used this stairwell. He expected to see a body slumped against the wall at every turn, not dead but not in any appreciable way alive, but there was only interminable darkness, the concrete stairs, his echoing footsteps.

The tenth-floor hallway was identical to the one downstairs but bookended by two small windows. Weak light stroking through the windows made the walls look darker, more desolate than the ones on the bottom floor. Reyersen walked to the end of one hallway, looked out the window. Half the buildings were taller than the hotel. He looked down on the old basilica a few blocks away, its limestone walls breaking up all the brick. He could almost see the harbor, in the process of being built up into some kind of tourist destination. As if that was ever going to work. He could see small local businesses and tall old buildings. The Masonic Temple. It was a city overlaid on a dark history. Enslaved people had once been driven through the center of the city, and, before that, the land had been ripped away from Native tribes.

Room 1021 had been discretely blocked off. Instead of ostentatious yellow caution tape, a simple seal covered the doorknob. Reyersen slid the blade of the putty knife he kept in his coat pocket into the slot of the door, jimmied the latch, slipped into the room, and closed the door behind him. He could have gone to the hotel management and explained who he was and what he needed to do, and they *might* have let him into the room anyway, but he'd been in too many situations where he couldn't get what he wanted by following official protocol. He did what he had to do to find out what he needed to know. He was a professional. Besides, he liked the risk of being caught, the frisson of potential danger. Part of him *wanted* to get caught. He'd been like that all his life.

An empty fifth of whiskey stood on the bedside table beside an ashtray full of five or six cigarette butts, smoked to the quick. None of them had lipstick on their filters. Beside the bottle and ashtray was a ragged paperback copy of a dimestore novel, *The Last Days of Lucky Lamore*. Reyersen pocketed the book.

The furnishings in the small room already looked dated. The accommodations would have been acceptable ten years earlier, but now they belonged to an earlier era—the world had changed since the forties. Gone ultramodern.

Supposedly. There was a fuzzy carpet under the chintzy bed. There was wall art featuring landscapes that were supposed to look grand and high class but only managed to look sad—some kind of country scene from three hundred years ago, back when there were natives and the land looked dramatic. The lighting in the painting was all gold and verdant green.

Reyersen settled onto the bed. Wholley had been wearing his raincoat, so he must not have been in the room long before "falling." He imagined Wholley, with his dependable head and features that didn't project any emotion, entering the room, sliding the whiskey bottle out of his pocket. Maybe it had been empty already. Maybe he'd spent the night before drinking in one of the seedy bars around Fells Point. It had been two p.m. when he fell/jumped off the balcony. Maybe a good greasy lunch would have saved him. Or a nap.

Reyersen paced the room. He walked to the sliding doors letting out onto the balcony. To call it a balcony was a kindness. It was a cheap structure, walking onto it at all an enactment of suicidal desire. The balcony was not even large enough for a folding chair. The only thing one could do was stand on it, smoking a cigarette, looking out over the city. On the day Wholley jumped, the city would have looked monochromatic. Dull browns, dull reds, dull grays. An ugly soup. The balcony looked like it had been designed for suicides. Reyersen imagined dozens of people jumping from their balconies at the same time, a ballet of human desperation. He imagined all of them landing with dull thuds, barely audible from ten stories up. The railing around the balcony was four feet tall, and Wholley would have had to climb it. There would be no accidentally tripping over it.

Suicide was the only reasonable option, besides murder, and there was no sign that anyone had broken into the room or that there had been a struggle.

Reyersen went back inside, settled onto the bed, his back against the wall. He crossed his legs and removed photos and files from the Manila folder. He had copies of the police report and all available public records about the man. Married for fifteen years. Two children, a son and a daughter. He'd lived in a suburb of Boston called Newton. Had been working for his company, which manufactured calculators, for twelve years. Aside from his wife and children, Reyersen didn't see how his absence from the earth made any difference at all. To anyone.

Reyersen returned to the office, a few blocks from the hotel, in the dead zone between City Hall and the construction around the harbor, to fill out the necessary paperwork. It was a blocky building built in 1912, and the rooms were small, his desk in an office crowded with three other desks. "Suicide," he wrote, in neat black letters, in the space marked "cause of death." He slid the report into his boss's inbox then made small talk with his coworkers, who were all waiting for the day to end. Janson and Hedges and Gray. None of them had any idea that Reyersen was recently married. He kept things like that to himself—not that there were many things like that. They talked about the start of the baseball season, the Orioles' chances, which were about nil, as usual, and the turn in the weather.

Then it was quitting time, and, as Reyersen walked down the hallway toward the elevators, all he could think about was Jayne, back at the apartment, waiting for him. At least he hoped so. Jayne would be wearing those pants that ended just below the knee and a shirt that tied around her stomach, an outfit meant for younger women, though Jayne could pull it off. In her early thirties, she was still in college, an undergrad, pursuing an anthropology degree. There was an about-equal chance that she wouldn't be at the apartment, that she'd be out drinking at the local bars with friends, or at the library alone, finishing a paper or studying for a test.

He was working on his jealousy issues, acting as if things like that didn't matter.

Reyersen had "met" Jayne while investigating another mysterious death, though that one had been cut and dried, in terms of the insurance pay-off. Her fiancé's head had been found propped on a log beside a trail in the Patapsco State Park. It was too bad they hadn't been married at the time, because Jayne would have received the poor sap's not inconsiderable death benefits. Instead, the money went to the victim's parents, who didn't need it. Reyersen wasn't sure what it was about the police reports that made him zero in on Jayne, but he'd read and reread transcripts of the interviews the cops had conducted with her. Something about the way she responded to their questions had piqued his curiosity. She'd been in shock, so nothing definitive could be said about her based on her responses, but there was a quiet stoicism to her reaction, a glacial calm he found alluring. He'd read all the news stories about the incident. Grisly murders were just starting to make their way into the newspapers. Unspeakable murders had always occurred, but at one time they'd been buried under a blanket of propriety. Now they were becoming fodder for the public. There had been a few photographs of the grieving fiancée in the newspapers, photos Reyersen had cut out in his apartment at night, a few stories meant to scare the squares, before interest in the story had waned. No one had ever been caught, and no motives were discovered for the murder and decapitation of Ted Graber, which was not as rare as people wanted to think. People got away with murder all the time.

Reyersen had found her address in the police reports. Easy as pie. At the time, Jayne had been living alone in the county, in an apartment complex that catered to single younger women, students, teachers, and nuns. He'd sat in his car watching the apartment for a few days before catching sight of her emerging from a back door. He couldn't say what it was about her—the pants that ended just past her knee, the way she walked? There was something about her, something both laden with the tragedy she'd experienced yet somehow lighter than air. He'd felt a keen urge to meet her.

He wasn't proud of the fact that he'd spent so long tracking her, and he was still surprised that his pursuit had produced results, that he had netted his quarry. It was not something he'd ever done before. For weeks he followed her, and when he wasn't following her he thought about her. She spent most of her time on the University of Baltimore campus, walking from building to building between classes, carrying books close to her chest. She was a regular at a coffeehouse Reyersen started frequenting—dark walls and hand-drawn advertisements for rooms to let and musical instruments for sale. There was often music and loud laughter, but sometimes, in the afternoon, there were lulls when the wannabe beatniks kicked back, sipping their coffees and writing pretentious verse in little notebooks. It was during one of those lulls that Reyersen approached Jayne as she sat by the window, gazing at the rainy street. He knew he looked like a square, with his button-up shirt, loose linen pants, and fedora, but when he leaned forward, looking at her out of a face that still bore the ravages of severe adolescent acne, he exuded a wolfish charm. He could feel it working on her. Sometimes it did.

They'd talked about Miles Davis, who was playing quietly over the sound system and had just released *Birth of the Cool*, a new direction for the musician. They had differing opinions on the album—he would realize later that she was right, that it was a step forward not a step back. Then they talked about artists, mostly older artists out of an earlier era, Man Ray, Mondrian, the Italian Futurists. Reyersen dabbled in drawing, had since he was an idealistic kid, though he no longer had serious aspirations. A doodle here, a doodle there. They talked about Jack Kerouac's *On the Road*, of course. Jayne wanted to be the next Margaret Mead, traveling, mucking through the world of ideas and the world of man. When she got excited about ideas, something inside her would glow out through her eyes.

Strangely, even when Reyersen was with Jayne he couldn't manage to see her clearly. He would forget what she looked like the instant he looked away from her. Her hair was on the edge of auburn. Her nose was not large, not small, straightish, her lips full-ish. Were her eyes green or gray? Sometimes one, sometimes the other. The light slid off her face rather than reflecting from it. He had never been so attracted to someone he couldn't see in his life.

They'd been married for exactly one week, following a simple ceremony at City Hall, his buddy Proster a witness. He never told her, and never would tell her, that their meeting at the coffeehouse had been more than accidental. Despite the fact that she was nearly ten years younger and more in tune with what was happening in the world of art and music, more *current*, and at least two times as smart, he was convinced they were meant for each other.

The days were getting longer, so light still clung to the edges of the sky when Reyersen walked to the bus stop outside City Hall. A dozen sad men huddled around the benches near the bus stop, all wearing dark suits under light raincoats. It was like stepping into a crowd of Ed Wholleys. They were all returning to their kids and row houses or suburban manses, the noise and clamor of family life. Reyersen thanked God he was free, had never taken that route. Propagation. Breeding. He and Jayne were in accord on that. No children. Some of the squares lived in the county, others in the middle class housing developments that ringed the city proper, housing developments with covenants to keep undesirables out. Some of them were probably Poles or Irishmen or Jews, but really they were all just gray men who commuted to work every day, carrying briefcases and wearing raincoats. Why did

Reyersen think he was any better? Maybe because he had a mind of his own, had not given up and thrown his lot in with the raging stream of sewage that was modern civilization.

Maybe.

He thought of the way Jayne had looked when he left the apartment that morning. Under the covers, she smelled like mushrooms and sunlight. Her hair over her face. Reyersen was no poet, but he found himself tempted to write poems about her. Which was a kind of sickness all its own. If someone had told him a year or two earlier that he would fall victim to love, he would have laughed in their face. But here he was, feeling the lack of something he was about to have again. Looking around him, he suspected the majority of men at the bus stop had never felt what he was feeling.

He wondered if Wholley had ever felt this way about his wife. He suspected that someone who decided to jump off a ten-story balcony must have experienced happiness at one point in his life. If there was no happiness, how could there be the kind of dejection that drove a man over a balcony? Reyersen pictured the big man falling, arms and legs streaming out behind him. The fall wouldn't have taken long. He wondered how many seconds it would take a two hundred pound man to fall ten stories. A mathematical equation. That's all it was, really. A question of numbers. A calculation. He felt sorry for the wife, who would now, thanks to a single word he'd written on a form, not be receiving death benefits, but that wasn't his concern. The jump, not the word, was the prime mover in that decision.

The bus driver, a gray and hunched old syphilitic he must have seen hundreds of times before, nodded at Reyersen as he climbed aboard, and he stood there, loop-hanging, watching the city pass, appreciating the way the light went lambent out the window. It was an ugly city, but the ugliness carried a kind of beauty along with it. It was mostly brick, but there were some already green patches of grass. Trees just starting to bud. By the time he got off the bus, across the city, it was dusk and then it was night and then he was walking through the night and he could taste her already. He imagined her spread out on the bed for him like a buffet. She had never done that before, presented herself to him like a gift, but maybe someday... A man could dream.

He lived in, now *they* lived in, what had once been an old clock tower, converted into apartments. He'd been living here for seven years, but returning to it now, when it held his new wife, it took on a different aspect. He liked the clock tower because it was tall and odd, and the apartments inside were large and open. Half were studios where artists either did or didn't work. There were often parties. The blare of hard driving jazz. This was what passed for the arts district in this small city. Weirdos and transvestites, beatniks and druggies, along with people who didn't fit and wanted to get away from the world—Reyersen, despite his square appearance and his square job, counted himself one of them.

He and Jayne lived on the second-from-the-top floor. There were two apartments on their floor, but the other one had been unoccupied for four years. The door to their apartment was ajar, which was not terribly troubling. Since the second was empty, no one ever walked onto their floor unless they were visiting, or lost. What *was* troubling was that none of the lights in the apartment were on. It surprised him that Jayne would leave without closing the door behind her, but apparently she had. Or else someone had broken in. When he walked in and saw the state of the apartment, Reyersen was not entirely sure someone hadn't.

Along with leaving the door ajar, Jayne had left the apartment in a state of disarray. A tan milk-crusted bowl sat on the coffee table. A coffee mug half-full of brown sludge. A bunch of books splayed out around the foot of the couch, textbooks and monographs. He closed the door behind him, trying not to feel annoyed, upset, or jealous. Living together was so new, he had no idea what to expect from Jayne. If he had to come home to a mess and an open door every day, what was the big deal? It was a fair trade, considering what he got in return.

The apartment's decor was eclectic. Reyersen had to admit to some wannabe beatnik proclivities. Most of the art on the walls was original, paintings he'd bought or bartered for from his clock tower neighbors. Sometimes artists had open houses in their studios and sold their work cheap. His favorite piece was a garish abstract behind the couch, a painting that looked like a gash of red blood against spatters of intestinal yellow. It made him think of life and death at the same time. He cleaned up Jayne's dishes and piled the books neatly, glancing at the titles. They were mostly anthropology books about Kwakiutls and Inuits.

In the bathroom, a pair of Jayne's nylons were hanging from the shower rod. Reyersen could imagine her gorgeous legs, substantial and shapely, ghosting inside. He crumpled the nylons in his fist and shoved his nose into the bunched material. He knew it wasn't right, the way he felt about her. The feeling of sexual mystery, of overwhelming erotic desire, was not the way a husband was supposed to feel about a wife. It was the way a middle-aged man felt about his young mistress, or the way a teenager felt about an older lover. He was bowled over by her presence, even the presence of her presence, the hint of her left behind. He felt raging desire. But there was nothing he could do with that desire until she got home. He had to bank it so he could stoke it later on.

He poured himself a bourbon, put the needle on the record that had been left on the turntable. Billie Holiday's "Strange Fruit" came bristling out of the speakers, the horns slow and dragging, the rhythm section plunking along. It was a haunting song, the music, lyrics, and vocals creating a dark mist. The deep darkness of U.S. history. The shallow shadows that infected all of them. "Southern trees bear strange fruit,"

Billie sang in her broken voice. It hit him and held onto his heart as he walked to the window to look out at the city. He was higher than Ed Wholley had been when he'd jumped off the balcony to his death. He could probably squeeze himself out the window if he wanted to, but, at least at the moment, he didn't have the faintest desire to do away with himself.

He awaited Jayne's return, awaited taking her up like a bad habit.

Billie stopped singing about the tragedy of U.S. history and started singing about love. "Love is like a faucet," she sang, coy and knowing. "It turns off and on."

Three hours later Reyersen was sprawled on the couch, a glass of bourbon on the floor, his head heavy, a bit deranged. He'd read the first third of T*he Death of Lucky Lamore*. The book was standard fare, about a gangster in a turf war with another gangster. There were pretty dames, rumrunners, and violence in spurts. He appreciated the aesthetics of the book, paid little attention to its plot. The characters were flat, but the atmosphere was rich. He knew Lucky Lamore was going to die, yet he invested emotional energy into the character anyway. Through the floor came the rumble of a party in process. The beating of percussion, maybe a blaring saxophone. Hard to tell. A comforting sound that would only get annoying when he tried to sleep.

In the bathroom, he put the nylons over his mouth and nose, breathing in, detecting the faintest trace of Jayne, while sitting on the john. There were atoms of her, her legs, her crotch, her ass, embedded in the nylons. No matter how hard she scrubbed them, she could never erase her scent. Now Reyersen couldn't hold back the emotions he'd been fighting all night. They flooded him, breaching the dam of his reserve, pressing against his eyeballs. Where the hell was she? What the hell was she doing, and who the hell was she doing it with? It was well past the time when she should have returned.

Even after being with her for almost a year, there remained things Reyersen didn't know about Jayne. There were great gaps in the history of her. Shadows and elisions. He had thought that was preferable to knowing everything about her. It gave him something to look forward to. He pictured her like a closed clam shell. He would pry her open eventually, sliding the edge of a putty blade between her lips, and reach in under the pink tongue that was her body. There were raw spots that made her recoil whenever he put his finger near them—maybe just the death of her fiancé (she never mentioned Graber), though he suspected something more fundamental. She never talked about her family, her childhood, where she'd grown up. She shared none of that with him. It was hard to tell if she had an accent or not. Maybe. He poured himself another slug of bourbon, settling his ragged breathing, then grabbed his coat and walked out into the night. The halls of the clock tower were dark and mostly quiet, but in the apartment one flight down the clatter of laughter and music sounded from behind a door. He knew a jazz musician lived there; he'd heard him practicing at all hours of the night, phrases bleating through a tenor sax.

It was colder outside now. This late at night, the buses were intermittent, at best, so he hailed a cab and headed to Fells Point. He and Jayne didn't make a habit of drinking in the bars out here, it wasn't their scene, but he knew some of her college friends did. The streets were cobblestone. Dozens of people staggered from bar to bar. It was cold, but, compared to how cold it had been a few weeks before, the weather made them forget it was still winter. Pretend to forget, anyway. There were dockworkers and fishermen tying one on, and groups of college kids making a nuisance of themselves. A volatile mix. Reyersen paid the cabdriver then walked the streets, hunched inside his raincoat and fedora. They probably mistook him for a fed.

He went into a hole in the wall and ordered a bourbon from a bartender with a red face and long blond hair. As he sat half-listening to the conversations around him, Reyersen realized how stupid he was. What if Jayne returned while he was out searching for her? He should have left a note. He had half a mind to return home and get back to waiting for her; instead he ordered another bourbon and looked around.

No way was Jayne going to be in a place like this, so he walked down toward the docks, where the more popular bars were located, and waded into the crowds. Here the ratio of college kids to working men evened out. They were insufferable. Most of them came from money and had no idea how fortunate they were. Beef-fed football players and effete intellectuals. In every group, Reyersen looked for Jayne's amber hair. A few times he thought he saw her, then he'd realize it was a younger woman, actually college aged. He imagined the interest the college boys must have shown in Jayne, an experienced woman. They were probably all after her. And Jayne too innocent to realize it. Maybe she'd been led into some dangerous situation, getting into a car with a half dozen young men with ill intentions. Rage spread through Reyersen's body, his ribcage, his arms, his fists. If he caught one of them, he'd pound him to a red pulp. Then again, he knew Jayne was too smart for that.

The night got away from him. His eyesight blurred. He got a drink only in half the bars he walked into, but even that was too many. He blurred and bleered and banged into beef-fed bodies that pushed back at him. He looked at the face of every woman in every bar, which he knew was putting him in danger. Someone was going to take it the wrong way. The women were shrinking violets and open white pages and sluts and saints, and not one of them was Jayne. He narrowly avoided a few fistfights. He didn't ask anyone if they'd seen her because he didn't have a picture and wasn't sure he could describe her. Average height. Brownish hair. Green or gray eyes. The description fit a million women. Yet somehow Jayne was singular.

When he felt something rising inside him, he scurried around the side of the docks to vomit up gray bourbon mash, and he breathed through his nose for a few minutes. The bay was before him, stars sliding off dark water riffled by wind. Across the bay, cranes outlined against the sky.

When he turned back around, he saw her, Jayne, scampering away, holding the hand of a college boy. It was just her back, the back of her amber hair, but Reyersen was certain it was her. Had to be. Though he didn't think she had a red dress like that. By the time he came to the mouth of the alley they'd disappeared down, he saw nothing. He was too drunk to be angry, too drunk to be sad. Still, he felt as if his entire life was spilling out from his insides.

He had no memory of making it back to the clock tower, his shirt and slacks miraculously free of vomit flecks. He still wore his shoes, not so miraculously clean. His hat sat on the bed like a bad omen. He groaned out a deep red bourbon-soaked bog, turned onto his back. Sometime during the night he'd gone through all Jayne's things, ripping her clothes out of the closet and strewing them around the room. It had been quite a bender. There were a lot of collegiate clothes, pants that ended past the knee, bobby sox, cardigans, but there were also professional-looking clothes, a pencil skirt he'd never seen her wear, a suit dress. There were a dozen shoes. Reyersen staggered to his feet before settling back down onto the bed, head pounding, mouth a wad of cotton. When he coughed, his heart squeezed inside his chest, like he had three fists.

On the floor was a shoebox he'd obviously rifled through the night before. There were a dozen photographs inside. An old black-and-white photograph of a family in the mountains. A father with a large forehead and a big grin wearing a suit. A dark-haired mother wearing a fur stole. A child that didn't look like a child but like a miniature version of the mother. He assumed the child was Jayne. Then there were photographs of, he assumed, Ted Graber. In one of the photos the young man was shirtless, smiling at the camera, cocky. Reyersen felt an instant dislike. He pictured the young man's head by the side of a trail in the woods, flies buzzing around his open mouth. There were a few photos of Ted and Jayne together. A series of three from a photobooth, mugging for the camera, their heads touching. They were so obviously in love it made Reyersen want to puke or cry, maybe both at the same time. There were letters Graber had written to her, but Reyersen was in no shape to read them.

Already late for work, Reyersen made himself a hangover special. Scrambled eggs with cheese, bacon, toast, the works. He put on the turntable and let the geometric jazz spread throughout the apartment. For years he'd been alone. He had never minded being alone. He could do whatever he wanted, whenever he wanted. He'd been a loner all his life. So why was being alone so hard all of a sudden? He had been with Jayne for less than a year, had lived with her for less than a week, yet somehow he felt like insects were clawing inside his skin trying to get out. Was it possible to change so completely, so quickly?

He was angry. Of course he was. She'd been gone all night without leaving a note. He hadn't heard word one from her. There had been no phone call. Nothing. He was angry, yes, but now he was also worried. He knew the kinds of unexpected, nefarious things that could happen to people out of the blue. Disappearances, murders, accidents. One second everything was fine, the next.... Men and women faked their deaths more often than anyone realized. There was an underworld of dark doings that, thanks to his job, Reyersen was privy to. What if Jayne had run across the wrong crowd? What if she wound up washed up in the harbor, her pale body bloated, crabs nibbling her entrails? What if she'd jumped from a balcony like Wholley, her hair streaming out behind her? There were all kinds of things he didn't want to imagine.

Most likely, she had simply wound up drinking too much at a girlfriend's apartment and spent the night somewhere. The time had got away from her. They didn't have protocols yet. Maybe this was how she was going to treat him—like an afterthought. He took a long hot shower, trying to push the dregs of his soul out through his feet, trying to stop the pounding of his head, then dressed in a clean white shirt and linen pants too thin for the March weather. He took a cab downtown, walking into the office two hours late. By the grace of a God he didn't believe in, no one noticed his tardiness. They probably assumed he was out investigating another suspicious death. It made him wish he'd slept later.

Two new files had been slapped on his desk. Nothing unusual. Nothing he had to investigate. Two simple, uncomplicated deaths. Most of his job was just this: routine paperwork, checking things over, searching for false notes that usually weren't there. Most deaths were perfectly explicable. Maybe once or twice a month he had to go out and do fieldwork, investigate shady dealings. He lived for those times, wished there were more of them.

The black phone on his desk rattled Reyersen out of his reverie. An angry jangling, the insides of the squat black box battering away. He lifted the receiver.

"Reyersen. Savor Life."

There was a pause over the line. He almost hung up. Then a voice started in on him. It was the voice not of a woman but of a harpy. It tunneled into his ear and sliced through his brain. Ed Wholley's wife. God, if this woman were his wife he would have jumped from a balcony, too. She told him she couldn't believe that the insurance company had the *audacity* to claim that her husband, who loved her and cared for her, who loved and cared for his two children, who were now without their father, would ever do such a thing as kill himself. Is that really what they were saying?

"I'm sorry, ma'am. The investigation is closed."

He hung up on her. When she called back, he took the receiver off the cradle, laid it on his desk, stared at it. It was a strange object, black and oblong. He could hear her voice coming through like a nattering insect. He pictured her in a tenement house, crowded onto a street with a bunch of other tenement houses somewhere outside Boston. He pictured a swarm of immigrant kids, some kind of Dickensian nightmare. When the nattering wore itself out, he replaced the receiver on the cradle. He looked around. Jansen, Hedges, and Gray had their heads down, working away at their own paperwork, or pretending to. It struck him that they were all extraneous, that if all four of them went out and did away with themselves—a gunshot to the head, death by train, jumping off a balcony or into the harbor—it would not make a whit of difference to the world. Not the faintest ripple would be felt.

In the afternoon he pretended he had a case to investigate, grabbing his hat from the hatrack, leaving the raincoat where it was. It was beautiful outside, buds unfurling, birds returned to the city in flocks. It must have been sixty or sixty-five degrees. He walked without knowing where he was going, until he realized where he was going. There was only one place he could be going.

The campus was mostly brick buildings, with greenswards here and there. They were all out in the warm weather, men and women barely men and barely women. Reyersen had not gone to college himself. Instead, he'd gone to war, an education in its own right. The Pacific Theater. Which was something he refused to think about, an unexplored region in his deep memories. Coming back, jaded, he'd found a job, then another. He'd worked his way up, until now he was a company man. Before the war, he'd been a reader, a budding artist, interested in culture. He'd gone to museums. He'd been soft, but the war had blasted that softness out of him. The people walking around him on the campus were still soft. Like marshmallow people. He could step on them and smooth them into the pavement. Many of the women, the girls, were attractive, but none of them held a candle to Jayne, and he barely looked at them. Their legs, their arms bared to the weather, their cupid bow mouths. He was too busy looking for Jayne to pay them any mind.

He remembered how he'd seen her everywhere he looked the night before, how every woman in every group had looked a little like her. Today, by contrast, none of the women looked like Jayne. They all looked younger, in every sense. They lacked her sophistication, the knowing way she moved her hips. He wished suddenly that he knew more about her, about the family in the pictures he'd found, about her time with Ted Graber. He felt like he had when he'd been following her, more than a year earlier. He had the same hopeless sense of hunt, the same endless hunger.

He walked into a few buildings, wandered down the hallways. He stood at the head of a lecture hall and looked inside at the tiers of seats. They were all lined up, listening to a professor with a beard and a tweed coat, a man who looked like a representation of what he was supposed to be. How could anyone live like that, Reyersen wondered? A shadow of the thing he was supposed to be? Then again, what was he? Anyone looking at him would spot him for an insurance man. And all the students were just shadows of students. The professor stood behind a podium rattling on about the initiating events of the Sino-Russian War. The man didn't know the first thing about war, had never been in one, had never *smelled* one. He was a brain in a case. He was nothing, really.

Reyersen walked down hallways that smelled like stone, then he walked back outside again. It was all pointless. There were hundreds of classrooms, and without knowing Jayne's schedule he'd never find her.

She was not in the coffeehouse, which was the same as ever, either.

It was shocking, how quickly Reyersen reacclimated to solitude. Already it felt natural to be alone again. When he returned from the office, early, the apartment still smelled like Jayne, but that smell would fade. He unwrapped the sandwich he'd bought on his way home from the office, opened the bourbon, sat at the table eating and drinking. His time with Jayne already seemed like a dream, half-remembered. Had they really been so hungry for each other? Had he really been able to bring her to completion, time and time again? Had they had happy times? Had it been that word they all feared, love? Maybe it was better that she was gone, because now they would never have to watch what they had fade. It would remain pristine and untouchable.

He listened to *Birth of the Cool*, again. Intricate lines moved inside the music. The instruments seemed to be saying something to each other he could barely decipher, talking in a language just beyond comprehension.

It was when side A of the record was over and Reyerson stood to return the arm that he noticed the bit of red cloth on a nail by the windowsill and noticed the open window. It had been open since last night, he realized. Had it really been open since last night? The apartment was always comfortable, heat rising from the other apartments, and he could often open the window even in the middle of winter. Now, in the lambent light of evening, he saw the bit of red cloth and felt something stick in his throat. Knew, already, even before he had moved to the window and looked down. Knew without any doubt.

The Bar Built in an Old Sheet Metal Factory

This was in Nashville, in the kind of rain you can't see through, a deluge.

I trudged up and down some streets until coming to the bar built in an old sheet metal factory, and there was the bartender with the neck tattoo and the pretty lady sitting there watching me as I walked in. The rain had washed off almost all the blood by then but not all the blood. Nothing washes off all the blood. She must have thought I'd done something irredeemable, but she was the kind of person who kind of liked that. Looked me up and down, said that thing about being dragged in by a cat.

Ordered a bourbon then another bourbon and drank them one after the other until my hands stopped shaking. Then I had another. It was loud as hell in there with the rain battering the tin roof. Sounded like it was still a sheet metal factory. Nobody could stay in there long without losing their minds.

I might have been concussed, was the thing. Couldn't keep my head straight. The bourbon didn't help any. I stayed there all night and might have left with the lady.

I had a big bump on my noggin the next day, but I was no worse for wear, and when I asked that bartender with the neck tattoo next time who that lady was was in the bar

last time he looked at me like I was crazy. Lady, he said? Wasn't no lady.
   I left it at that.

The Feeding

Pierre sat looking at the second dead person he had ever made dead. Shot through the chest, a gaping wound that bled all over the tile floor. He recognized the guy, was surprised to find him here dead on his kitchen floor, never would have suspected anything like this from him. On the counter his phone kept buzzing. The groupchat, a bunch of cop buddies, was popping off. It was 5:00 on a Thursday evening and some of them wanted to meet up for a happy hour but couldn't get their shit together. None of them could ever get their shit together, which was why they were all buddies. The smell of cordite invaded his nostrils, made him want to sneeze.

Pierre found himself stuck in the paralysis of consequences. Thoughts crept into his mind—who was this guy again?, a small-time drug dealer?, someone he'd put away? no, a former high school classmate, that's who—but he wasn't thinking them. They skated along the surface of his frozen mind. Clean-up had to be considered. It was going to be a bitch, but he'd testified at enough trials to know exactly how to clean his mess without being detected. The body another story.

The blast from the .357, not his service weapon but one of his personal stash he'd happened to be cleaning, thank God, when the guy burst into the kitchen brandishing his own piece, a Glock held to his side like some action movie hero, had opened up a gaping hole, and now that the smell of cordite was dissipating Pierre began to smell the man's inner body odors. Smells he'd smelled plenty of times before. A beat cop, he wasn't generally called to homicide scenes, but he'd been at plenty. The odors were overpowering, stenchy, shit and rot and iron and other things no one had any reason to ever smell. The damn phone kept vibrating on the counter, text after text from a bunch of jokers whose biggest problem was figuring out where to get drunkest cheapest.

He wondered why the guy had tried to off him. Someone must have paid him. What remained of the guy looked rough. Maybe he needed a fix, the old scourge heroin, or Oxy or whatever the fuck. He was dressed in an old flannel shirt and a dirty t-shirt, jeans held up by a belt cinched too tight. And he hadn't been handy with that little peashooter by his side. An inexperienced hitman. Todd P was the guy's name, it dawned on him. What the P stood for was anyone's guess. He wondered why Rusty hadn't alerted him to the presence of the intruder.

It was mid-November but in the fifties, and he opened the windows to let in some fresh air and let out the stench of opened body and cordite. Put classic metal on the Bluetooth speaker. Motörhead, "Ace of Spades." Wondered if any of his neighbors heard the gunshot but wasn't worried, gunshots not an uncommon occurrence in the neighborhood.

Motherfuck the body had made a mess. Guts on the tiles, guts on the counter, guts slime-trailing across his cellphone. He wiped it clean with a dishrag. The boys were meeting at Roper's out on 111 at 6:00. He got a tarp from the bed of his F-150, a silver truck shining in the sun surrounded by dull leaves that had once been yellow and red but were now brown and rust. Smelled the fresh New Hampshire forest all around. Felt an instinctive flush, winter not far off, hunting season. Rusty's body was tied to the three steps leading to the rancher, tongue like a pink sponge peeping out between dark lips. His ribcage still.

Pierre felt a darkness that sometimes took him over completely moving inside him. The son of a bitch had poisoned his dog then watched him die. It made what Pierre had done to the body, the gaping hole, more forgivable. Righteous, even. No man who poisoned a dog deserved to live. He unclipped the dog's leash and dragged him around back of his trailer. Then he bent over, hands on thighs, and cried. When he was done, he patted the dog's ribs and went back to get the tarp.

The body did not roll. Deadweight, 170 pounds if he had to guess, and Pierre not the biggest guy in the world—5'2" 130 soaking wet. He managed not to spill the insides any more over the kitchen floor than he already had. Wrestled the body, the black tarp rolled out on the floor. He could already taste the Rolling Rock at Roper's, feel the tension of this escapade spooling out of him as he laughed with his buddies, flirting with Misty, the waitress who still wouldn't give him her number.

Finally, he got the body wrapped tight, duct-taped the tarp closed, dragged the body out of the kitchen, leaving a smear of blood on the tiles. Heart bounding, arms protesting, the front door banging against the body, the sun suddenly too hot outside the trailer, the sound of Motörhead giving way to Iron Maiden, "The Number of the Beast." The body was heavy, and it had been a year since he'd lifted weights. His back twinged as he tried to get it up onto the bed of the truck, finally able to jimmy it up there and let the weight carry the rest of it forward.

In the bed of the pickup the body looked like anything else wrapped in a tarp. Just something to unload at the dump. Easiest, maybe, to bury him in the woods behind the trailer, but Pierre was smarter than that. No fool, Pierre LaCoeur. Too close, and the woods weren't as deep as they looked. A mile in and you'd reach the back of the Hannaford. More action back there than you'd expect. Kids doing drugs, shooting .22s, fucking if they were lucky. Homeless guys in cheap tents where they could dive the dumpsters.

One thing Pierre had learned in life: the easiest way to clean a mess was to get at it right away. Don't let anything set. So he went at it, taking all his cleaning supplies out from under the sink, listening to a cavalcade of metal classics, from Black Sabbath to Anthrax to Megadeth. Shit he'd always listened to, would never stop listening to. Headbanger for life. He scrubbed and scraped, the sudsy water in the gray bucket turning maroon, dumping the bucketfuls out back. He wore yellow plastic gloves, scrubbing up little pieces of Todd P, the poor fool who thought he could off Pierre LaCoeur without repercussions. Fuck with Pierre and reap the whirlwind.

Rain had started by the time he made his way out of Roper's, a few sheets to the wind, raindrops tapping the tarp in the F-150's bed. Inside Roper's it had been all beer and music and darts and flirting with Misty, who flirted back but only enough to ensure that he tipped well. He was pretty sure he was in love with Misty, a schoolboy infatuation anyway. He liked her too-long face, a face that kept her from being out of his league, and the way she wore shirts that opened in front, giving a little show every time she leaned over to rinse a glass. Liked her crooked smile and the way she laughed at his jokes. There was just something about her whole vibe. He was sure half the guys at Roper's felt the same way but was convinced there was something special between them. Some day he'd make a real play for her. Not tonight.

He sat in the warm cab of the F-150, listened to the rain pattering the plastic tarp. Imagined DNA leaking out the bottom of the tarp all over the bed of the truck. He had to handle this tonight. Inside Roper's he'd thought about bringing Santos into it, but every time he almost said something Santos made a joke or told another story, and Santos had a million of 'em. No, he was alone in this. Even though he was pretty sure whoever had sent the fucker to kill him had done so because of what he'd gotten into with Santos. That whole mess.

He headed toward the northern section of town—deep dark woods. Drove past the entrance to some newly built developments, out into backroads without streetlights, deeper dark in the rainy night. Turned off between two boulders, the F-150 climbing the rocky road like a truck commercial, Pierre like he was sitting atop an elephant tossed this way and that, the body in the tarp sliding and slamming into the side of the bed. As teenagers, they'd come up here to drink, and then he'd brought girls up here to fuck around. A rough dirt road ending at a flat rise overlooking White Lake. They'd jumped into the lake from here, twenty feet down.

Turning off the engine, sunk into the deep darkness of a night swallowed in sepulchral rain, Pierre let it take him for a second, a raft he floated out on. Half-drunk and calm, yet he also felt the reality of what had happened earlier that evening come sit on his shoulders like a demon in the night. What if he hadn't been cleaning his gun? What-ifs could be crippling. What was was: he had killed another man. True, it had been him or Pierre, and no way Pierre was going out like that, but there were consequences for every action.

Getting out of the truck, hunkering in the cold rain. Opening the back gate of the truck and dragging the body to the edge of the bed. Even heavier than before. He dragged the tarp to the bed's edge, the weight of the body bringing it to the ground with a thud. Dragged it closer to the ledge. Opened the tarp and larded it with random rocks.

He dragged the weighted tarp to the edge of the cliff, cautious, knowing how easy it would be to let the weight of the body carry him with it, imagining a little Pierre flying through the air. Then no more Pierre anymore. He felt something tweak in his lower back as he hefted the body—three hundred pounds now?—and somehow manhandled it so it was flying end over end the twenty feet into White Lake. He could see it, a darker blackness than the black night, then he couldn't, but then he heard the splash and spe-lonk like a huge rock.

Back at his place all he wanted to do was get out of the wet clothes, slide under some covers, and sleep, but then he remembered that he forgot about Rusty out back. His poor dumb dead dog who deserved better than to be abandoned in the back of his trailer. He huddled like a little gremlin as he made his way around the trailer to deal with the dog's body.

Stopped around the corner. Not expecting to see what he saw. Some dark shape settling then unsettling from the body, unfurling like a thousand crows and scattering like shadow, and he wasn't even sure that he had seen it, because the next thing he knew there was nothing but the dog's body, opened now. Something, *something*, had been feeding. The dog's ribcage showed, bones wet and white, innards glistening.

Got a shovel from the plastic shed in the corner of the yard and went out into the dark woods, his eyes adjusted enough that he could discern rock and root. He settled for a flat spot behind the shed, began digging. His thrown back allowed him almost no leverage, and he worried he was going to slip a disk, but he had to get the dog's body hidden, safe from the predations of whatever shadow creature he'd seen when he turned the corner, which he knew was not real but some figment. He stopped and took a piss and got his breath back, looked down and saw that he'd hardly even started a hole. It was turning out to be a long night.

A couple hours later he dragged the dog's body into the hole and covered it with a few stones, a protective layer, then dirt. He made a mound and stood, his lower back on fire, like a series of steel cables being pulled through the flesh. He said a couple words over Rusty's grave, not dust to dust but words of salvation and gratitude. Rusty a good old faithful beast who deserved manumission in the afterlife. Succor.

Inside, it felt both stiller and more animate than usual, like there were several hauntings going on at the same time—Todd P, the dumb asshole who'd tried to kill him, his faithful old beast Rusty, and whatever it was that had been feeding on Rusty out back of the trailer. They crowded inside the kitchen, which reeked of bleach and blood.

Morning. Rain again. The dancing perorations of his cellphone alarm, stupid twinkling shit that always pissed him off enough to wake him up. The pain had settled so deep in his lower back his coccyx felt like shattered glass. Pierre levered himself up out of bed, rocking a little, wincing and moaning.

Each step an excoriation. Payment for a life of venial sins, with a few mortal ones thrown in. In the bathroom mirror, was that him? His face ashen, eyes underlined with black bags. He was a full-ass adult with the face of a little kid, but suddenly he looked like an old man. Opened the medicine cabinet and found a baggie of percs they'd stolen from some wastoid they'd collared—back when he was working with Santos, before Terry Simpkins, who was a do-gooder.

Popped three percs then limped into the kitchen, eating a frozen waffle. So quiet in the house without Rusty it felt suddenly emptied. The pain in his back was, thank God, abating, the percs working their magic.

Put his uniform on, looked at himself again in the mirror, a little better but worse for wear for sure. Everyone had a bad day sometimes. Even Simpkins, though he had yet to see it.

When he walked around the trailer to check on the burial site of his beloved dog, he was not surprised but a little horrified to see the grave ripped open, the rocks thrown aside, what remained of the dog's body half in and half out of the hole. Its guts were gone now, the remains nothing but a skeleton and hide, Rusty's big dumb skull. He kicked the dog's remains back in the hole and covered him over again with rocks and a layer of dirt, even though he knew there was no use to it now. There were claw marks from some unearthly beast in the dirt around the grave, paws bigger than any paws he'd ever seen. Something was feeding on his dead dog, growing stronger, a dark shadow creature out there in the dripping woods. Gawd. He wiped his hands on his black uniform pants and went barrel-assing down the street in his F-150, only fifteen minutes late.

After his shift ended—a mercifully slow day driving around town doing fuckall—Pierre drove to Roper's, where only day drunks drank, Misty behind the bar wearing a black shirt with a boat-neck scalloped out to show her breastbone. His heart beat like a dying mule. She was surprised to see him.

"Pierre LeCoeur," she said.

"Misty..." he smiled. He wasn't sure if it was still Higgins.

"You here on business?"

"Naw. Just got off duty. I..." He wanted to tell her he'd wanted to see her too much to waste time going home and getting changed but didn't.

She slid him a Rolling Rock and he sat nursing it, watching her, the TV above her head playing a classic baseball game from the 80s—he recognized Dennis Eckersley. Misty kept glancing his way. A man in uniform. Maybe. He hoped. She was different around him. He felt more comfortable in the uniform than he would have in his street clothes, armored. "What time you get off tonight?" he finally asked.

"What time do I get off? Why?"

"I'd like to take you somewhere."

Crooked teeth showed in her smile. "I get off at nine. Where do you think you're going to take me at that time?"

"Good question. Up to White Lake?"

She smiled, shook her head a little.

"Sure, Pierre LaCoeur, come back at nine and take me to White Lake."

He nodded, sucked down the rest of the Rolling Rock, a yeasty lukewarm mash at the bottom of the green bottle. It was only when he stood that he remembered his bad back. It screamed, almost forcing him to his knees, but in the F-150 he took a couple more percs and breathed through the pain.

He was parked in Roper's lot at 8:45, listening to *Master of Reality* and steeling himself. When she finally came out, Misty was wearing a camouflage coat and a black beanie and she looked tired, but when she saw him sitting in his F-150 her face lit up. Was it possible she felt the same way as he did? Hard to believe but not impossible. People could be fooled by all kinds of things.

She slid into the seat beside him.

"Haven't been up to White Lake in years."

"Yeah?"

"That's where all the boys would take me when they wanted to get in my pants."

"I will neither confirm nor deny…"

"Oh, I know what you want. But that doesn't mean you're gonna get it."

He let the words layer themselves in the cab like smoke. Neither of them had any illusions. It was easier than it had been when they were teens but still not easy. He could make a wrong move any moment and everything would fall apart. Crumble like old cake.

Up the rocky road to the overlook, he and Misty now like two riders of elephants riding the swales of gravity. He felt her smiling. Maybe she didn't get out enough.

At the clearing he turned off the engine and they sat in the animate darkness. He wondered if the thing in his backyard could follow him out here, the being of shadows that could break apart or agglomerate itself, one being or two dozen flittering beings. One big-ass monster or a bunch of bats. Wondered if he were leading her into danger.

He could see the scuff marks on the ground from where he'd dragged Todd P's body but knew Misty wouldn't notice. They set about gathering rocks and arranging them in a circle, then they gathered dead branches and kindling. He appreciated a woman who could work, didn't need to be told what to do. The duff was damp, but underneath the top layer were dry pine needles and old leaves. They collected small branches and larger fallen limbs. Pierre was pleased to see they were making a big pile of wood; they both planned on spending some time out here together.

Before long the fire blazed. The night was entirely animate around them, but then it shrank and crouched to the size of the fire's nimbus. They sat on a flat log staring into the heart of the fire. No need to rush anything. They had all night. He thought of Todd P's body falling through the night, landing with a splash. Thought of it wrapped in its tarp at the bottom of White Lake. Wondered how many other bodies were buried down there.

"This is nice," he said, after a while.

Misty didn't respond, didn't seem capable of responding, her soul sucked out by the fire. He wondered if she was not who he thought she was but some revenant returned to enact revenge.

He sat beside her until finally becoming comfortable with the silence. Watched the fire barely thinking, the time passing on cat's paws. Until she turned toward him. Strange how the fire made it seem as if her skull was empty and something burning behind her eyes.

"Do you have a gun with you?"

"Of course I have a gun. I'm a cop."

"Let's see it."

"You want to see my gun?"

"I want to see your gun."

He walked back to the F-150 and opened the glove box, took out his P229, magazine inserted, safety on. It was a simple gun, sleek in its design. When he returned, Misty had moved off near the overlook and stood waiting.

"I want you to shoot your gun for me."

"You want me to shoot my gun?"

"Yeah."

He shrugged, clicked off the safety, extended his arm. The gunshot loud but dissipating quickly, almost comical in the open space above the lake. He felt the aftereffects of the shot in his arm, heard a ringing in his ear.

"Now let me shoot it."

He shrugged, handed her the gun, their bare hands making contact for a second. Felt immediately the malevolence of the barrel as it was pointed in his direction. Realized his mistake, handing her the instrument of his own death. Her eyes were hard and her face was hard and all he felt was a hatred born of no source he could discern concentrated on him. For a second he considered not reacting, letting her shoot him, ending it all, but then he took a step back and his foot was scraping the edge of the overlook and he was sliding down, and she was above him—he heard the gunshot just above his head, heard the whistle as a bullet passing close to his head, and he was scrambling to find purchase on the cliff. Luckily he was on the side where there was some purchase to be had and he was landing in bushes and his back was on fire and he was running hunched over through the woods, his heart lolloping. *Just run*, he told himself.

After a while he stopped running and stood still in the woods. All he could see from the overlook were snaking arms of light from the fire. Misty was not following, but he sensed her awaiting his return. He could outwait her. In the woods away from the fire, it was cold, the newborn winter fierce and already settling into the land where it would reign for the next five months.

When he came to the bottom of the hill near the entrance to the dirt road, he tried to decide what to do. Was surprised to see his own truck come barreling down the road, humping over rocks, Misty at the wheel. He crouched, but she was not looking for him, fishtailing onto the road, the truck and Misty gone.

He thumbed his phone on and ordered an Uber, waited by the side of the road until an old man with a white mustache wearing a Red Sox cap picked him up.

He got out at his trailer, hobbling around back, every step like something being pulled out of his lower spine. Of course the gravesite of his dog wasn't intact, earth flowering out of the hole like a bloom, and now the dog's carcass entirely gone, as if bones and scraps a last-ditch meal for whatever incarnate beast was out there.

Inside, he grabbed his .357 and took off his pants and unbuttoned his flannel shirt. He couldn't maneuver to get the undershirt off. Took the last three percs in the plastic baggie and lay in bed. The tears that came unbidden from inside him were sourceless, or their source so deep and dark he refused to plumb that source.

The darkness of a dream shattered the second he woke but left random images behind. Woods, beating wings, the blast of a shotgun, Todd P's body cavity beating as if his whole body were a heart. Pierre shook the images away, tried to move but couldn't. Only his head and neck capable of any movement at all. The rest of him unresponsive under a lattice of pain.

The twinkling of his goddamn phone alarm started, and within a minute he was losing his mind. The electronic cascades went on and on. It was seven a.m. and it was hard not to count every second until it was 7:15, the alarm still sounding. No matter how hard he tried, he could not get his arms to function. He wondered if he was a quadriplegic for life. Didn't think so. Had just pushed himself too hard the last couple days.

He was more concerned about losing his mind than with whatever was wrong with his body. The alarm still twinkling away, the sound boring into his brain like an insect. He felt his bladder prodding him. Motherfuck it was a bad morning all around. Had been a bad week.

When the alarm suddenly cut out, the cellphone battery dying, it was a sweet relief but also the harbinger of a greater sorrow. The house felt haunted, and the land outside the house, the woods just beyond the wall of the trailer by his head, felt even more haunted. Things were waiting for him to move so they could devour him. Something, or a conglomeration of many little things, was waiting outside.

Hours passed in idle contemplation of his earthly existence. Couldn't call it thinking. It was waiting, ignoring the prodding of his bladder. If he waited long enough his muscles would start working again, would respond to messages sent from his brain. Just had to be patient. Pierre LaCoeur not known for patience.

He tried to get some momentum going, moving his head left and right, but his body was a lumpen thing, an anchored weight on the bed, and when he tried too hard pain attacked from several directions at once.

And then Santos, somehow, was standing over the bed. Pierre had not heard an engine, or the door opening. Maybe he'd fallen asleep without realizing it. Santos's head was disproportionately large, though he was, Pierre had to admit, handsome.

"The big detective," Pierre said.

"What are you doing in bed this time of day, bud?"

"I can't move. Hurt my back. Got any percs?"

"Percs? Do I have any percs? No, I don't have any percs, buddy." Santos looked around the room. Piles of clothes in corners. A *Kill 'Em All* poster on the wall.

Santos knocked a bunch of clothes off an easy chair and sat, crossing his legs, regarding Pierre as if he were a suspect. Pierre did not like it at all.

"You're really in a bad way, huh?"

"I can't remember being in a worse way."

Santos nodded, smiled, and for a second he looked like the old Santos, Pierre's buddy. The trouble they'd made together. The shit they'd gotten into. Some of it legal, some of it not. Santos was the one skimming money. So what, they stole from criminals? Santos wore a cashmere sweater and a silk shirt. In the past few months, he'd transformed from a regular guy into whoever this guy was. He'd spent a lot of the money they'd grifted.

"It's been a rough couple days. People are trying to kill me."

"People?"

He shrugged as best he could, a wave of pain rolling down his back.

"Remember Todd P? From school?"

"Todd P? Sure, I remember Todd P."

"Son of a bitch broke into my trailer yesterday, the day before yesterday, tried to shoot me."

"Is that right? And where is he now?"

"I got the jump on him."

"You got the jump on him. That doesn't answer my question. Where is he now?"

"At the bottom of White Lake. Wrapped in a tarp." He smiled but Santos didn't smile back. Santos nodded, looked at his watch again.

"I gotta get going, bud. I'm supposed to be investigating a homicide up north. You know Misty Higgins? Shot through the heart with a P229. Pretty girl. Bartended at Roper's. I know you remember her."

"Sure," Pierre said. He felt himself shrink inside his useless body. He watched Santos leave the room, and after he was gone he was not sure he had ever been there.

Days were already starting to shorten and Pierre felt shadows gather around him like crows on a tree. He'd pissed himself and the smell got bad and the cold got worse and then the smell went away or he got used to it and the cold settled into his body but then it got worse, too. It was almost unbelievable how much he missed his dog; he thought of the walks through the woods he'd take with Rusty, the warmth of his body in the bed with him. He missed no person he'd ever lost in his life but missed his dog like crazy.

A light rain had started to fall. Now as the day edged into night he heard raindrops freeze like tiny teeth tossed against the siding of the trailer. He felt addled and his throat was drier than it had ever been. Like he'd swallowed a fir branch. He'd slept off and on throughout the day but dreamlessly, as if his brain were not capable of making images anymore.

In the depth of a darkness that had no end because it had no source, Pierre sensed more than saw shadows creep toward him. Winged but silent. They moved on crouched legs like frogs but had no locomotion. They gathered around him. Then he was aware of the darkness covering his eyes, a light pressure and an impenetrable darkness darker than the absolute darkness. Other shadows stopped up his ears until the silence was profound. As if he were in an anechoic chamber. He could no longer even hear the beating of his heart or the shushing of blood in his veins, and it was a greater terror than anything he had ever experienced. Would if he could move, spasm, throw the shadows off him, but his head and neck were now as incapable of movement as the rest of him. His nostrils were next, stoppered with shadows like black gauze until he couldn't smell or breathe through his nose, only his mouth left agape like some sightless eye. Then that too covered with a shadowy film.

Everything Rises

It rained for five days straight. Dead things got deader. Creek folk hunkered inside their houses, peering out from pale faces. Pierson stood by his window watching water wreak havoc with the land. He'd been living in the holler for fifteen years, had arrived out of nowhere and bought the old Rash place. He lived alone, made his living in a way none of us could fathom, maybe doing something online.

I'd been watching Pierson for about half a year to that point. Curiosity, force of habit: call it what you want. I used to do reconnaissance. Haven't done much of anything for some time.

Once a month, Pierson drove out of the holler in his big green Range Rover, old enough to fit in with other vehicles around here but still a damn nice vehicle. Once he'd cleared the holler, I'd waltz down to his place and do a little snooping. There were old photos in a shoebox let me know Pierson had once had a family. Good looking big boned wife. A son with a head too big for his body. He had a Smith & Wesson Performance Center Model M&P R8 case made me think he might have been police at one time and made me wonder where the actual gun was at.

He'd always come back late at night, when it was too dark to see what he was doing. He'd work under cover of darkness.

The rain was hard and heavy, and for the first few days no one minded it. That kind of downpour was normal this time of year, though it swelled the river and threatened to flood the houses closest by.

By the third day everyone was well sick of the rain, surly. We'd turned into a bunch of grouchy bears. It was the time of Pierson's monthly trip out of the holler, but he didn't go anywhere. I saw his face hovering by the window. Pale but not pale like the rest of us. A special pale.

On the fifth day of rain, everything waterlogged as a drowned dog, I watched Pierson walk out the front door of the old Rash place, but not moving toward his Range Rover the way he normally would. He wore a modern brand of rain jacket, was all bundled up in a watch cap and black boots. He looked up and around the way a guilty man does before walking around to the side of his place.

I fetched my hunting rifle and followed a small game trail to get a closer look.

After a while, I noticed the well was overflowing, water seeping up from out of the dark hole usually covered by a metal plate. The metal plate had been pushed away from the hole by the force of the water spreading all over the yard. Everything rises after a while. You wait long enough and everything comes back.

Pierson stood back from the well watching it overflow, obviously expecting something.

And then it happened. The earth disgorged its dead, or rather *his* dead: one body after another, naked as the day they were born, men and women and children, a whole grotesquerie of them, a few dozen bodies at least. They were all pale but some of the oldest ones were blue and as soaked through as cranberries in a cranberry bog. Body after body came up, splurping out of that well, gangly-limbed, their knees and shoulders like burnished knots. I was sure they'd all been shot in the head, by that Smith & Wesson no doubt.

Pierson sat there watching them come forth from the earth, probably wondering how he was going to stuff them back down into it.

I realized as I watched that those bodies were not just bodies, they were people who'd lived in the towns within a three hours' drive of the holler, with their own problems and passions and peculiarities.

The waters just kept rising. I had a decision to make: call the cops or handle the business on my own. You can probably guess that we have no need for the law up here.

Night Moves

It was dark by the time Joyce left Bon Secours, the edges of the horizon holding on to the last pink flicker of sunset, and she felt like a used dishrag. She needed to be wrung out, drained of all the dirtiness she'd absorbed throughout the day working at the hospital. Her feet throbbed. She'd known when she left in the morning that the shoes would cause her problems, but she didn't always want to wear sensible shoes. Sometimes the price of a little pain was worth knowing you were still a flesh-and-blood woman. And she'd been complimented on the shoes, half heels with a button strap across the top, three times that day—by two women in the transportation department where she worked and by a volunteer, Sandeep, who must have been all of twenty-five. She had noticed but never paid the slightest bit of attention to Sandeep before, but on one of her many trips on the elevators he'd looked foot-ward and she saw his eyes widen, his breath coming out a little more forcefully. The telltale signs of arousal.

"Oh, I *love* those shoes," he said, almost despite himself. And she didn't know exactly what he'd been picturing, but it had been... sexual at the very least. He was not a bad looking young man, with neatly parted black hair and a trim mustache, almost debonair, and for half the day she pictured him in compromising positions, her mind a boudoir. She was somehow sure that he had a powerful upper body, dark brown perfectly defined pecs and biceps, though she'd only ever seen him wearing long-sleeved button-ups, even in summer. The imagining hadn't been tied to anything that could ever happen in the real world. No, it was just a way to pass the time and make her feel better about herself—at least *someone* wanted her. Not real, yet it produced a very real throb somewhere other than her feet that she knew Jack back home was not going to satisfy, that, if there was any satisfying to be done, she would have to do herself. Take a shower and frig herself hard and fast, bring forward the flush of quick and complete orgasm. Though that wasn't what she wanted, not at all. She wanted to linger. She wanted someone else to linger on and over and in her. She wanted waves of pleasure to ripple through her body. For hours. The way Jack had once made her feel. And she was sure Sandeep, sweet kind debonair Sandeep, would be more than willing, more than capable. Give him a chance and away he'd go.

It was dark in the parking lot, even darker in the far lot where she'd parked the fifteen-year-old AMC Pacer that had once been Jack's pride and joy and was now Joyce's shame. Pee-yellow where it retained color at all, where Bondo wasn't slapped across the body in gray smudges. It still ran well, she had to give it that. It purred, sending vibrations through her throbbing feet and up her legs. 'BCN blared on, that Standell's song they were always playing, "Dirty Water."

In the white shock of the headlights, she saw, across the lot, the shape of some animal hunkering by the old stone walls that encased Bon Secours. A raccoon, she assumed, but when it turned to look at her she saw the white visage of a possum. Its teeth tiny and pearlescent. Its eyes strangely human, as if it were judging her, looking deep into her soul and finding her wanting. Or wanton. It saw the lust in her heart. It had been so long since Jack had even touched her, and he had an excuse for not touching her. She wanted nothing more than to run the thing over, crush its skull under the tires of the Pacer.

She was tired and hungry was all it was. Her long day toting patients around the hospital exhausted her. Patients on stretchers or in wheelchairs. Spending time between calls in the tiny office where four to seven people sat all day smoking cigarettes and listening to the Iran Contra Scandal on the portable radio, Louise, her boss, the softball playing dyke (she meant no offense; Louise called her own self a dyke) nattering on about this and that politician that meant nothing to Joyce. Getting hit on by Stanley, the old white-haired volunteer, who complimented other things besides her shoes, every damn time he saw her. He tried to hide it by using old-fashioned phrases. He liked the cut of her jib really just meant he liked her tits. She'd spent the day smoking Virginia Slims between trips. She hadn't eaten anything since lunch, roast beef sandwiches someone had brought in from Harrison's. A long day, no matter how you cut it.

She wished she didn't know exactly what she would find once she got home, exactly where Jack would be and what he'd be doing. She drove out of the lot and onto the back roads to the west of Bon Secours, the streets without streetlamps, everything dark and wild as if they were in deep wilderness not Methuen, Mass. She couldn't shake the afterimage of the possum's pale face. It was tattooed, all white, on the back of her eyeball. That slithering grin. Those eyes that weighed and found her wanting.

She drove down unlit backstreets until she came to their neighborhood, a codicil of ranchers just south of the New Hampshire border, parked the Pacer in front of their white rancher, turned off the engine. It rattled an extra few seconds, the way it always did, turning over like it was reluctant to let go, like this might be the last time. Joyce slung her bag onto her shoulder, walked in to find the exact scene she'd expected. The light was on in the kitchen, spilling into the unlit living room, where the flickering images from the TV illuminated the room in green, white, and red. The Red Sox, up three in the 8th inning. Jack sitting in his customary recliner, his one remaining leg extended, his stump freed from the unfurled bandage, red and raw-looking in the green light. Jack's eyes not dissimilar from the possum's when he turned to acknowledge her existence, that same sense of judgment.

"Hey Jack," she said, unsnapping and kicking off her shoes, her dogs letting out almost audible yips of relief. "Bad day?" She motioned toward the stump. Jack made a gesture between a wince and a shrug and turned back toward the screen, where Oil Can Boyd was being replaced on the mound by Bob Stanley.

It was true that he'd lost his leg only three months earlier, in a motorcycle accident that had seen him sprawled across the highway like roadkill, and that that kind of thing would affect anyone's libido, but he hadn't lost his third leg. Just the ability to use that third leg for anything other than to piss, loudly, against the porcelain john, every few hours, day or night. He had not gone back to work—he was, or had been, a master mechanic at the Chevy dealership—had not even talked about what he might do for work next. He had started filling out the paperwork for disability but hadn't been able to finish even that. He hadn't touched her once since the accident. She'd been tempted to just grab his cock, but for some reason she didn't want to be the one to initiate things. She wanted to be wanted. Was that too much to ask?

"You want me to rub it?" she asked, in a way that would have elicited a different reaction three months earlier. Back then he had still liked to back her up against the wall and fuck her standing up. Even after years, their sex life had been wild and rough, both of them almost always ready for a go. He had liked to take her on the couch. Liked to get rough, but only as rough as she wanted him to, as if he could read her mind, unlike other assholes in her past, who either went too far, leaving bruises, or didn't go far enough, not leaving any marks at all. He was perfectly brutal and sweet in equal measure. She missed that Jack.

"No," Jack said. "Thanks."

She changed into sweats and a t-shirt, made herself a Stouffer's pizza in the toaster oven. The possum face was still in her mind. Strange how perfectly she could see it. She'd always assumed all possums looked the same, but the one in her mind was an individual. Something about its eyes. She wondered if there was something wrong with her brain. What if something far worse were to get stuck in it? Wasn't that what happened to psychos? They lost control of their minds.

She ate the pizza while Jack slept in the recliner, the Red Sox blowing their lead and the game going into extra innings. She did not give a single shit about the Red Sox, or any other team. It seemed dumb to expend energy as an adult worrying about young men who dressed up in costumes and played with balls. Sometimes she liked to watch the men, admiring their physiques, but tonight she didn't. Quiet as she could, she put slippers on and snuck out the front door, careful with the screen door so it didn't slap back in the frame. She walked around back. Their small yard was overgrown. Joyce had mowed it herself, for the first time in her life, about a month earlier.

A little stone wall enclosed the yard. Beyond the wall, what looked at this time of night like stark wilderness but was only a few acres of woods. She climbed over the stone wall and found herself in shadow. She could hear the drone of crickets and thought of the possum face. There were probably dozens of possums out here. Raccoons for damn sure. She saw deer now and then. Plus the smaller creatures of the woods: toads, snakes, birds. It was warm but not hot, a cool breeze presaging autumn. In the moonlight, she saw the creek running, rills around stones, and she stepped across it and entered the deeper shadows on the other side. She had rarely been out here.

When she couldn't see their house, she stopped walking and leaned against the trunk of a big old tree, snaking her hand into her sweats. She could already smell her own desire, that smell that would have no impact on Jack but would get Sandeep revving. She pictured him in front of her in the woods, shirtless, his muscles taut. She pictured his cock hard and perfect, eight inches long, imagined guiding it inside her. Wrapping her leg around him, the bark rough against her back. She would teach him what her body needed, how, where, for how long, until he figured it out on his own and didn't have to be told anymore. She didn't stop until she had come three times, and when she pulled her hand out of her pants she could feel her pussy vibrating.

The next day at work she wore a striped red and pink shirt with a plunging neckline and heels. Jeans that molded to her legs and ass. She knew her body was not for everyone, but it had an appeal for men who were not afraid of some heft. It definitely had an appeal for Stanley, the old volunteer, who made no secret he was staring down her shirtfront every chance he got. "What are you *doing* to me, darling?" he said. She wanted to tell him to fuck off; she wasn't doing anything to him.

The heels were not stilettos, but they were higher than she would usually wear to work. Bright red with a little sparkle to them. When Sandeep finally got onto the elevator with her—she was transporting an old woman whose pink scalp was visible through wispy white hair—he seemed not to see her at first. But when he looked down, his eyes widened briefly and his nostrils flared, as if picking up her scent. A hunter of very willing prey.

"Beautiful," he said. And that was all. They exchanged quick glances and smiled at each other, and she felt the chaotic lightning of longing pass between them. It had been so long. She imagined rolling the old lady off the elevator and trapping them both inside the little space, imagined him tearing at her clothes, holding the shoes in his hands, putting her legs up on his strong brown shoulders as he entered her. She let her imagination go wild, the throb that had already started in her feet finding a corresponding throb in her pussy. When he got off the elevator to go to his volunteer gig at PT, she watched him, imagining him naked, strolling like a god down the hallway.

He had not paid the slightest bit of attention to her cleavage, which caused her all manner of problems all day, the men she transported never feeble enough not to sneak a peek. One man, Mr. Hurlihey, flat on a stretcher, reached his hand out to grab her tit. He was on his way to a CAT scan and could barely open his eyes thanks to a stroke, but give him a chance to stroke her tit and he'd take it. It was wrong to fault them for holding on to their desire. Since Jack had not touched her once in the last three months, everything seemed imbued with desire. Dripping with it. The old people no less frisky than the young ones.

Sitting in the transportation department office, Joyce smoked cigarettes and tried to listen to the Iran Contra hearings—she didn't care; she really didn't—the droning voices a backdrop to her vivid imagination. How different would it be with an Indian man? She was not bigoted, she didn't think, but she had grown up in an environment where differences were more ethnic than racial. She was Irish and Italian while Jack was Irish and German. Irish, German, Portuguese, Italian. Her high school had been mixed in that way. She had not met an actual Indian person until she'd met Sandeep, and she couldn't say she'd really met him at all. Had no idea what he might believe or eat or what kinds of holidays he celebrated.

That night another Red Sox game, the other Stouffer's, Jack falling asleep with his stump swaddled like a baby, not such a bad day for him, another slipping out through the door and lingering on herself in the deep dark woods, her fingers sliding and slipping and rubbing, her breath caught in her throat and a feeling of exposure and risk and deep need that was not being alleviated by the masturbation but was in fact being stoked by it. As she was walking back toward the house she saw an animal on the stone wall. Again, she assumed it was a raccoon, and again it was a possum. As she got closer, it stopped still and stared at her, its tiny teeth little points of moonlight. That creepy humanesque face.

She was afraid of the possum in the way people can become afraid of statues or churches, as if it were animate evil. The stillness was a defense mechanism, and it didn't move as she made her way around it, climbing the stone wall quickly and hurrying across the back yard. When she turned to look, it was gone, back, she assumed, into the dark wood.

On her days off, she would go to the mall or the outlet stores up in Kittery and look at shoes. She didn't always buy the shoes, but too often for their bank account she did. She bought heels and strappy sandals, kitten heels and boots. She hid them from Jack, but he seemed incapable of curiosity anymore. He'd gained fifteen pounds since the accident. A sheen coated his eyes. She wondered what would happen once baseball season ended, but she had all of October to worry about that.

The boots. Did they go too far? *Were* they too much? The second she saw them in the store in the new Rockingham Mall she fell in love with them. Head over (ha ha) heels. They were everything she had ever wanted in a shoe. Sexy but not slutty. Half boots with half heels. Bright yellow cheetah print, textured like fur. They were the kind of boots models wore in hair metal videos, but they were also classy.

She wanted to wear them all the time, but she wore them only once to work. She felt taller, sexier, statuesque. She wore a black turtleneck, because it was finally getting cooler, tight jeans, and the cheetah print boots, and she felt everyone's eyes on her. They were too much. But she didn't care. One of the other women in the transportation office asked if she had a hot date, Stanley had to wipe drool from his chin, even the softball playing dyke couldn't hide the fact that she was attracted to the boots. At first Joyce was self-conscious, but then she said fuck it. She didn't care anymore. A little attention never hurt anyone.

And the boots had the desired effect. She heard Sandeep's breath catch in the elevator.

"Those boots," he said. She wanted to grab his head and mash it against her tits. Wanted him to grab her ass. Wanted to joust with him there in the metal box of the elevator, which had always seemed sterile until the past few weeks.

"Do you like them?" she asked, her voice, rough from cigarettes, coquettish.

"Oh yes, I like them."

And she wanted, desperately, to figure out a way to keep the conversation going, to draw him in. She felt like a spider, he the fly in her web. Yet she couldn't figure out how to sustain the conversation, not with the old man, who had an IV next to his wheelchair and smelled like bleach and old man shit, next to her. Sandeep smiled.

"Have a good day, Joyce," he said. The first time he'd ever said her name. How did he even know it? Oh, her nametag. She trembled a little. Found herself smiling at odd moments. Would she really throw away her marriage just for a roll in the hay with a beautiful Indian boy? She was pretty sure she would, yes.

When she returned home, Jack was in the kitchen getting himself a beer. She took the boots off, placed them side by side beside the door, where six other pairs of new shoes were lined up, in order of sexiness. Heels and straps and bright garish colors. Together like that by the door, did they look desperate? She took a quick shower, dressed in an oversized t-shirt, came out to see Jack leaning against the back of the couch, holding himself up with his hands behind his back, and looking at the array of shoes. She could feel it in the air: realization. But what was he realizing, exactly? What did he *think* he was realizing? The usual, probably. An affair. She was so dumb. Of course he was going to suspect something was up. Any sudden change could be seen as suspicious.

She sidled up next to him.

"It's been so long, Jack," she said. And she reached down and took hold of him through his shorts. His third leg responded, the way it always had: a reassurance. She took it out and got on her knees in front of him. He was still looking at the shoes, but after a few seconds he grabbed the back of her head and looked down at her. After a minute or so of getting him ready, she led him into the bedroom. They tried it with him on top, but he couldn't find purchase with the stump, and he winced and his erection lost its rigor until she guided him onto his back. He didn't usually like her on top, but he was hard and ready and he grabbed and pawed and growled deep in his throat. She closed her eyes, imagining Sandeep.

Afterwards, they lay in bed a while. She felt the ocean of sensory perception recede from her, as if she were bare rock. She pictured the smiling head of a possum. She felt the presence of Jack beside her, his big dumb manbody, the girth around his waist bigger than ever. His stump didn't bother her. It was a new part of him that she could learn to love, if he only let her.

"Get dressed up in those new boots of yours and I'll take you out to dinner," he said. "How's that sound?"

She wanted nothing more than to laze around the rancher. Do nothing. Have a beer. Maybe watch a movie—they still had two they hadn't watched from Blockbuster yet. One of Jack's picks, one of hers, an action movie and a rom com. She didn't want to go anywhere, but the fact that Jack wanted to get out of the house was so momentous she didn't dare turn him down. Who knew when it would happen again. She dressed in a pleather skirt and a dark blue top—Jack liked skirts, and the boots went perfectly with the get-up.

She drove the Pacer, parking it on a side street in the old downtown of the mill city. There were hills that would be hard for Jack to navigate with his crutches so she parked as close as she could to Gracie's, a dark little restaurant overlooking the Merrimack River. The first place he'd taken her, that he thought, with his limited experience in matters of the heart, was romantic. A working-class Massachusetts kind of romance, she supposed. It looked and felt the same as always as she walked and he crutched through the bar, people calling out to him. "Jack!" He grinned sideways, roguish. He'd been roguish in his youth. Petty crime. Fistfights. Before he'd settled into his job at Chevy, where he'd worked hard to become master mechanic. She'd almost forgotten how well-loved he was, how many "buddies" he had. Maybe he was clinically depressed. Maybe she should cut him some slack.

Sitting there at a two-top by the window overlooking the Merrimack, Joyce thought of the possum. Maybe now that he'd fucked her, she could finally get over this feeling she'd been having lately, the lust, but instead it had ignited a slow burning in her lower stomach. She just wanted more, and not necessarily from Jack. He looked paler than he'd been before the accident, bigger. He seemed limited in important ways that she'd never let herself notice before. They ordered beers and sandwiches and sat trying to think of what to say to each other.

It was in this bubble of mutual discomfort that she noticed Sandeep across the room. The throb went off in her like a small bomb and she worried Jack would see it, but at first he didn't. He was oblivious. Sandeep sat at a table with three friends, two of them Indian, the other white, maybe Italian, with slicked back black hair, biceps bulging out of his t-shirt. And Sandeep was wearing a t-shirt for the first time, and what she'd suspected was true. He had such strong arms. His biceps bulged like two dark brown sexy sausages. She tried not to stare but couldn't help herself.

Finally Jack noticed her looking and turned to see what had her attention. She was sure he was going to sense it, her attraction, but instead he sneered.

"What is that? A fucking sand nigger?"

She felt something strong and alive, like a small animal, tear at her heart.

"Jack, don't say that. I know him. I work with him. He's a smart kid. He's going to become a doctor."

"There's a surprise." Jack turned around and focused on his food.

She felt desperate to catch Sandeep's eyes, but he was lost in his own world, with his friends. Then she noticed the other man reaching for Sandeep's arm—not the way a friend reaches for another friend's arm. There was familiarity there. They were familiar with each other's bodies, in a way that made her mad with jealousy. She felt so stupid tears flooded her eyes and she could barely breathe. The cheetah print boots were stupid. She was stupid.

"I like him," she said. And Jack, to his credit, realized something was happening because he reached across the table, squeezed her arm, and looked into her eyes.

"Okay, Joycee," he said. "I'm sorry. I'm sure he's a good guy. I'm just being an idiot. You know me."

They ate and drank. Jack drank beers and shots men from the bar kept sending over. They would come over and shake his hand, grab him by the shoulder, laugh with him. Reminisce about nights when they got so drunk they couldn't talk, nights when they spelled their names in piss in the snow. They asked him where he'd been and how he was doing, and not one of them mentioned his leg or looked at his stump, ignorance a kind of tenderness. He was so loved. Joyce was glad to see it, and she tried to let the feelings slide off her: the disappointment of the mediocre sex that afternoon, the realization that Sandeep was not attracted to her, only liked shoes, the fact that she would be stuck in Methuen for the rest of her life, her unanswerable desire, the coming of winter. It all bore down on her, but she did her best to ignore it.

Jack was well drunk by the time they left Gracie's. Flushed with the adulation of his peers.

For some reason she was not ready for the night to end.

"Let's drive to the fort," she suggested. "Can we, Jack?"

"Sure, Joycee. Drive us anywhere you want." He was being magnanimous. A small-town king.

The fort was on the coast, a place they used to fuck and hang out before they had a place of their own. She turned on 'BCN to find "Night Moves" playing. She loved that frickin' song. It seemed like a sign, fate, something, and she turned it up and sang along, loud. "Strange how the night moves, with autumn closing in."

The Pacer was small and crowded, and Jack was snoring by the time they were out of town. Joyce drove down snaking back roads without streetlights, feeling something gather inside her. Bob Seger was replaced by Pink Floyd, then by Led Zeppelin. "Going to California." Good, familiar songs, one after another. She lit a Virginia Slim, cracked the window, the bite of autumn through the window, and felt alone. The possum grinned in her mind.

She parked off Route 1 on the Coast. She rooted through the hatchback of the Pacer, finding some flipflops that had been there since they'd gone to the beach the summer before. This summer had been nothing but a drag, with Jack in the recliner all the time, her working all the time. She took off the boots. The cheetah print in the moonlight. She half-wanted to throw the boots onto the street, into the dunes, into the ocean, but she had a sense she would need them again, soon. Her bare feet felt cold but sumptuous in the flipflops.

Roused from his drunken stupor, Jack groaned like a bear.

"Come on, Big Boy," she said. He came to slowly. Tried to smile at her. This was their special place. Just a little walk through an overgrown path. To what had once been a World War II fort, when the Navy had monitored the ocean for Nazi warships. The coast was broken here, rocky and wild. The waves thrashed against the rocks like something trying to get free of something else.

Jack was awkward on his crutches, but he negotiated the path to the fort. Concrete abutments. This was the first place they had ever fucked. A place they came back to now and then to remind themselves of who they used to be.

She climbed to the top of the fort, the overgrown roof twenty feet up where a few scurfy trees held on, and where they could see to the edge of the ocean. Jack followed slowly, awkwardly, heaving his body on the crutches. She knew he was only doing it to please her. That she should cut him some slack. How many times had they fucked on this roof? A hundred? It was a place they felt exposed and hidden at the same time, where it felt like they were risking something.

She listened to Jack panting. He had always been on the large side, and now he was obese. The possum flashed in her mind. The boots. Sandeep with his lover. The faces of all the old folks she carted around the hospital, taking them to tests and therapy and sometimes wheeling them to the hospital lobby so they could be released. There was something so human and vulnerable about them all. They'd all had their chances and either blown them or taken them.

She waited until Jack had climbed up next to her and was by the edge of the roof before pushing him, heaving with all her might, her flipflops finding purchase on the roots of desperate trees. Above the sound of the wind and the thrashing ocean, she heard something snap—his good leg?—when he landed.

He was still calling her name when she got back into the Pacer and drove away.

Butch

We wait in the unemployment line. The guy in front of me has a bodybuilder's body and a blond crewcut, just like me. We wait for a long time, looking at the back of the head of the person in front of us.

Then, fed up, me and the guy start pounding each other's shoulder blades—boom! boom!—over and over, like a toy where you pull a string. I don't know who started it. We butt our heads right against the other guy's shoulder, clasp our hands, raise them up, then jack-hammer them down. Man, it feels good.

We become buddies.

He steals my girl, I steal his girl.

When I fuck her, I picture him fucking the other one, and it's like fucking two girls at the same time.

We have achieved the impossible.

I carry a pocket magnifying glass with me everywhere. One day he falls asleep on the beach and wakes up to a bush fire in his chest hair. Ha, you lousy bastard, I yell. He beats at the fire with a paw like a large rock and just glares.

A few months later I wake up at a friend's house after a party, my toenails painted pink, lips smeared red, eyes this garish sparkling blue. Some joke, I say. He calls me Nancy. I have to hide my boner—wherever that came from.

Sometimes we bang into each other like we're in a house of mirrors. Sometimes we laugh, other times we push each other away. Sometimes we butt our heads into each other's shoulders and pound away—boom!, boom!—breathing like bulls, like Muhammad Ali, the Rumble in the Jungle.

Who is this guy, my mother says. I don't like him, I don't trust him.
Then he brings her a Tupperware container full of chocolate turtles he made. When we're leaving, she kisses him on the cheek and leaves a smear of brown.
I love this fucking guy, she says.
Was it just the turtles, I wonder.

To substitute for not having any work, we smash things with baseball bats. Old TVs, obsolete computer equipment, junkers that we steal from the street, sometimes driving them back with sparks flying from their rims. We hold our rifles against our well-developed shoulders and target practice with the canned peaches my mother gives us. Later we throw them at each other. The mason jars crash and spatter, thick syrup running down our chests, coagulating in our chest hairs.
We buy a big dog and the dog licks the syrup off us. We call the dog Butch and laugh because his head is a perfect cube.

I watch him sleeping sometimes and it's like I don't need to sleep myself. I've taken up origami. I make him a little paper AK-47 and plant it on the pillow next to him.

And, of course, there's the working out.

We should start our own fucking war, he says, because we missed ours. Too young for the Gulf. He stares out the window wistful at the dying lawn.

Wait a while, I say.

We take Mom out for her birthday to some fancy bar where an old guy sings Frank Sinatra karaoke. The guy wheels around an IV machine and seems about to die. We order sushi and talk about our new dog and Mom's hormone treatment.

Then, at nine, they start the strobe lights and the dance music. It's like another whole place. He asks Mom to dance. Watching them, it's all I can do not to throw up my sushi. I swear to God she sticks her tongue in his ear. His huge hand rests on the small of her back. They are both laughing.

Everything's a fucking tragedy to you, he says.

We're close, in the hallway, and I pound him on the shoulder blades. Bam! Bam! I want him to fall on his knees, but we're too evenly matched. He's the same body type as me. We've been doing the same workout routine. Boom! Boom! I should get him drunk and do this, I think. Then we'd see who went down.

A fucking tragedy, he says again.

I drive his truck, he drives my truck. It doesn't matter. Sometimes we drive together, flipping other drivers the bird, yelling at the faggots, the losers, the morons who don't know enough to stay out of our way. This is our road, motherfucker.

Butch is incontinent and it's always me who's cleaning up after him, holding an old workout shirt to my nose, scrubbing with the special foaming spray. Butch gets the shakes at night and it's always me that holds him until he stops. Leave it to us to buy a dog with a terminal disease.

Poor, beautiful, dying Butch.

I get into the shower and start lathering before I realize that he's in there already. He narrows his eyes and smiles. He looks at me and I look at him. He is so blond, so cut. I only hope I look as good.

He steps out of the shower, leaves me alone.

Hey, I say. He smiles when I smile. He raises the same eyebrow I do. Then I realize that that's not him, that's my reflection in the mirror.

Back from the unemployment office, I find Mom in a black evening dress that's not like anything she'd usually wear, lying on the kitchen floor with Butch, who's panting raspily. He smells bad. Like death.

Mom's crying.

Your dog's dying, she says. And I'm so fucking old. Her hair is mussed and her face is lobster red. Upstairs I hear the shower going. He's singing something. It takes a second to place it. Frank Sinatra. "I've Got You Under My Skin."

I just stand there. Maybe the smell is not death, I realize.

He makes me a nice Caesar salad, watches me eat it.

Good, I say.

He shrugs and looks away. What's happening here?

I wake him up by punching him in the face. He just looks at me. Then he punches me in the face. I take a jar of peaches and pour the syrup on his chest. He lets me rub it in. Then he knees me in the crotch and I knee him back.

I start bumping into walls, windows, mirrors. I'm like one of those birds that fly into the picture window. Dazed. I sit up with Butch, but I'm not sure anymore who's shivering and who's comforting.

I remember the good times, like fucking his girl and pounding him on the back, shooting jars, smashing an old TV, riding around in his or my truck.

You don't have to call me Dad if you don't want, he says.

He wrestles me onto my back. His breath smells like a strawberry daiquiri. I wrestle him onto his back. We punch each other's faces. He's wearing a tux, for god's sake. Talk about tragedy.

Butch gets worse and worse, but I still don't believe he's going to die. I start bumping into Butch, because *he's* gone to Cancun with Mom.

I have three job interviews scheduled for Monday. I decide to shave my entire body. Afterwards, I look at myself in the mirror, and don't see him anymore. I look smooth and natural.

Idiotic American Boys

His beard grew longer. His hands roughened from working in the cold. He split wood for hours in back of the house, where his grandfather had left chunks waiting to be split. He sharpened the ax head on the whetstone his grandfather had taught him how to use. His blood thickened. Sometimes he still shivered in the cold but less often now. It snowed. It was January, if not February. He lost track of hours, days. He stood on the dock while the sun set over the lake, feeling the air gather around him and disperse.

He walked to the eastern end of the island often, somehow comforted by the broken land, then he walked back. He saw deer. Sometimes they scattered at the sound of his footsteps, but more often now they just lifted their heads to watch him. The herd, apparently permanent to the island, seemed to be growing. Maybe they had always wintered here and he just never knew. He imagined shooting one, slicing open its soft belly and hanging it, waiting for the meat to turn from red to peach pink, slicing into the carcass. Flank steaks, saddle steaks, ground beef. He imagined gorging on meat. But he had not hunted since he was a teenager, and he refused to shoot a deer with a handgun.

He put off returning to the mainland for supplies as long as he could. He could survive on canned goods until April, but he could not survive without coffee. He went one day without and his body protested, his head aching. If he had to, he could pass through the need, but in the early morning he bundled up in his heavy jacket, his thermal shirt and pants and jeans, his gloves and fur-lined hat, and he set off across the frozen lake. The sky was still dark, darker because overcast, everything solid gray. He felt like he was setting off on a long, dangerous trek, when all he was doing was crossing the lake for supplies.

The lake was so large it was hard to believe the whole thing could freeze, but the ice was solid underfoot, and when the sun rose high enough and broke through the cloud-cover he could see colors in it, mostly pale pinks, purples, and blues. Air bubbles. The surface was rough, embedded with tiny sticks. Fishing sheds, tiny plywood houses on runners, had been dragged onto the ice near the other shore. A few of them were occupied. He felt like a man coming out of deep wilderness, even though he'd only been on the island alone for a couple months. Some of the men in the fishing sheds raised their hands. They held mugs of coffee or rum. There were children sitting on little folding chairs or sliding around the ice. The men sat over holes filled with deep black water like nothingness.

The Chevy Sonic was in the parking lot where he'd left it. He wondered if anyone had spotted it yet, reported it as abandoned, checked its provenance. One of its tires was flat. He walked past it. It was midday but still very cold by the time he got to the library. When he entered the warm lobby, he swooned and took off his gloves and hat, blinking and breathing slowly. The proximity of other people had become strange to him. It *was* possible for a tame animal to re-wild. He was slowly shifting away from the need for human connection. If it were possible to stay on the island, and if it were always winter, he could leave them behind forever.

He signed up for an hour on the computer. At first he sat before the monitor unsure what to do. The whole network felt doomed. If he wrote one word it could suck him back in. He opened his Gmail account and found an email from Priya. It asked him where he was and whether he was safe, claimed she was worried about him. He suspected a trap, imagined police monitoring her email account, waiting for his reply, ready to track him. He typed his three-word reply—I'm fine, thanks—and sent it anyway, then sat regretting sending anything. He had been so careful until now.

He remembered their first kiss in the parking lot of the high school, her body close to his, before they'd fallen completely into it. How mixed his emotions had been, the struggle to maintain order giving way to desire. How fraught it had felt—but delicious and inevitable. Love. He had never believed in it until he met Priya. She was different from anyone he'd ever met, but she felt familiar. That was the least of his problems now. His fingers looked too large, clumsy on the keyboard.

He refused to think about the things he'd done, had successfully blocked them from his conscious mind until now. Was not going to allow them in, though shards of memories pressed like glass against other memories. Hannah with her sleep-puffed face that morning. The heavy emptiness of Priya's apartment when he left it. He desperately wanted to go back to before, but there was no before.

He typed in the name—"Brian Sanderson"—and found an article about a man who'd been arrested for several murders in the area. In the accompanying photo, the man looked indigent, his hair wild, his jaw dusted with stubble.

He bought a large bag of coffee and a half-gallon of milk, a bag of Doritos because he missed the rich fake flavor of junk food, a package of individually wrapped cupcakes. He bought a large bag of white rice, pasta and sauce and a baguette for his dinner that evening. Everything fit, barely, inside one paper bag he carried cradled under his arm. He felt happy to leave it all behind, the town, the people, and return to isolation. He would not return again until spring arrived and people started using the lake more often. He had no idea what he would do then. Maybe head west. Maybe return to civilization, if that were possible. All he knew was that he was happy to head back to the island. He would worry about the future when the future came.

He walked past the men and their children in fishing sheds, almost certainly drinking rum from their thermoses now. He heard laughter, and then he was away from them, alone on the lake. The silence and isolation and space. The edge of the lake went to the horizon. He had to walk slowly on the ice. Winter birds flew in the distance, too far away for him to identify.

He did not hear the young men following him until they were upon him. When he turned, alerted by the sound of ice crunching, a thick piece of wood, a chair leg or baseball bat, caught him across the side of the head. He saw faces covered in ski masks, bodies in dark clothes. He went down, blacking out even before he had time to wonder who they were and why he had not brought his gun. Not that it would have done him any good.

In dreams he had plotted to have his wife killed. He hired two men in suits without faces to do away with her. He thought they would do it discreetly, but they arrived in the middle of the night, while he was still sleeping, stumbling up the stairs, banging against the walls, making no attempt to be quiet. They pressed a pillow against Hannah's sleep-puffed face, raised fingers to the space where their lips should have been, then, their no-faces turned toward him, shot her, the silencer and the pillow swallowing all sound. Rivers of blood seeped from the edge of the bed. He would jolt awake, soaked in guilt, turning over to look at the humped shape of his sleeping wife. He had not intended any of this. He didn't want to hurt her, nevermind kill her, though apparently part of him wanted to do just that.

He knew he was going to have to leave her but wasn't sure he would be able to. Hannah was the first woman who ever loved him. When he met her he'd been coming out of his drug days, crawling out of darkness, twenty-two years old, unlovable. She'd helped him come back to himself, had encouraged him to go back to school, had supported him while he got his master's, had believed in him when no one else had. She'd talked him through the difficult decision to leave the Army Corps of Engineers and take up teaching. In his own way, he loved Hannah more than he had ever or could ever love anyone. An abiding but tempered love. He was sure that, at this point, she needed him more than he needed her. Leaving her might kill her, would definitely destroy her. She didn't suspect a thing, thought their lives were, if not perfect, at least set. He wasn't sure she could recuperate from that kind of trauma, wasn't sure he could put her through it. She had given him Casey, their daughter, in her final year at college. They had raised her together, true partners, and he was proud of her. She was an incredible young woman. How could he throw all that away?

Stephen came to slowly, climbing out of thick darkness, the knot on his head throbbing. It was not like waking from sleep, was more like resurrection, coming back to life, gasping for breath. He tried to move, but his torso had been tied, tightly but inexpertly, to a straight-backed chair. He tried to determine how injured he was, to take stock of the situation. Blood coated the left side of his body. Then he realized it was not blood but tomato sauce, the thick red liquid glinting with slivers of glass from the broken jar. Aside from his throbbing head, he couldn't detect any injuries. He was in the family house on the island, where he'd run away from what he'd done, tied to a chair, in the shadows under the loft, so far from the fire he couldn't feel it, his breath pluming before him.

There were people in the house with him—the young men who'd knocked him out, he assumed—and the smell of frying garlic. He could see their bodies but not their faces in the kitchen. They were shifting shadows. Always in motion. His father's bottle of single-malt scotch stood on the counter, almost empty, surrounded by brown beer bottles. Dead soldiers. Someone grabbed the scotch and drank from it. He heard the rough, hurried laughter of young men, always in competition with one another. He had been like that once, too—wild. He had pushed against expectations. Had smashed shit. He could not parse their sentences as they talked over each other. There were at least three of them. No more than five.

One of the young men crouched before him, a ski mask covering his face, so close Stephen could smell the alcohol on his breath and feel strands of wool from the mask against his face. Neither of them spoke. The young man's bloodshot eyes had dark centers. His smile showed jagged eyeteeth. He was frightening because he was so normal. Like someone Stephen might pass on the street without noticing.

The young man pressed his index finger against Stephen's temple with a slow, steady, incrementally increasing pressure. Then he stopped, the force of the pressure remaining as he turned and walked away. He wore tan work boots and thick black jeans.

After their fling was over, apparently, their run of motel rooms, where they fucked with abandon, ended, they saw each other in faculty meetings and sometimes in the hallways between classes. Priya smiled and nodded as if he were any other colleague, a fellow adult in a swarm of teenagers. They ran into each other on Friday afternoons drinking with other science, math, and social studies teachers but kept their distance. Or he did, sitting on a stool as far from her as possible. She had stopped texting him. Was, as his students would say, "ghosting" him. Would not return his increasingly desperate texts. He tried to stop thinking about her, to let her go. He felt like something had been ripped out of him. Some future happiness denied him. How could she not feel the same way? It had always been mutual, hadn't it? Of course it hadn't. How could it have been? He was not up to her level. She had been playing with him the whole time.

Since Hannah had been the first real relationship in his life, he had never experienced this before. It seemed absurd, beyond sad, to be experiencing this kind of pain, "heartbreak," at his age. He was almost fifty years old, for God's sake. At the beginning of the affair, he couldn't think about anything but Priya, imagined talking to her all the time, and now he still couldn't stop thinking about her, but there was nowhere for his thoughts to go. There was a scientific term for this kind of problem. What happened to energy that couldn't spend itself?

One night at the bar of the "American Bar and Grille" where they met for drinks, he overheard that she was seeing someone, that that was why she no longer met them for drinks. Now he caught sight of her only in the hallways or in the teacher's lounge, where she said hello, as if he were any other fellow teacher. Apparently she'd forgotten she told him that she was in love with him, too.

He heard them eating in the kitchen, heard them slurping up pasta, heard the clatter of forks against plates. The smell of the food induced both hunger and nausea. His head ached and he felt like a man in an underwater cage, figures just beyond his sight range. Sharks, whales, submarines, creatures that were not named and had never been seen before. Out the window the sun set red over the lake. The sunset, often brilliant, was even more brilliant tonight. It looked like the world was ending, but of course it was only the day.

In almost total darkness, they took up baseball bats they'd brought with them. At first he thought they were going to hit him with the bats, were going to beat him to death, but they ignored him, took the bats to the interior of the house instead.

They yelled and laughed as they destroyed. One of the young men grabbed Stephen's guitar from its case and smashed it against the floor, wielding it above his head before bringing it down. The strings held the neck and body together momentarily, wood shattering. When he threw the pieces of the guitar into the fire, veneer blistered. They threw cans of soup against the wall as hard as they could, making a game of it, denting the wood, some cans cracking open and oozing. They laughed, held bottles of beer, lifting the masks from their mouths to drink, though that didn't help Stephen identify them. They were indistinguishable young white men, resembling frat boys, baby fat and stubble on their cheeks. Idiotic American boys. They smashed against each other, smeared each other with beef stew, yelled, chanted, cheered each other on. They were out of control, and yet part of it was just for show.

They laughed and talked and yelled, and one of them played music out of a small speaker, the music rough-edged, from another world, a world of dark streets and hard days.

They all pissed inside the house, two of them in the corners and one of them directly in front of Stephen. The young man had lowered the mask over his face again, and he took his dick out and sprayed urine six inches from Stephen's feet, a steady stream pattering on the floor, his eyes on Stephen the whole time.

"Hey," *he said to the boy* who was slumped over in the hallway not far from him. The boy was wrapped inside a sleeping bag. It was like looking at himself from when he was a child, though he knew the boy was a teenager, maybe twenty. He looked younger, wrapped in the sleeping bag. When his head emerged, Stephen couldn't see his face in the darkness.

"What?"

"Do you have a family?"

"Shut up," the kid said.

"I get it," he said. "I get what you're doing. I might have done the same thing back when I was your age. Tearing shit down. Right? Sometimes that's all you want to do."

"Shut up," the kid said again.

And so he did. He heard the kid's breathing get regular and even, and then he was asleep and Stephen was alone. He wasn't any different than the vandals.

He sat outside on the front steps of their townhouse in a t-shirt and jeans, staring blankly at the small lawn, a rake leaning on the steps beside him. Small piles of brown leaves dotted the lawn. He could barely move, every year of his life suddenly taking on weight. He checked his cell phone again. Priya had not answered his last text, or the dozens before that, but he sent another one anyway. *I miss you.* It was so sad, so bald, so true, that after he sent it he deleted all the texts they'd ever sent each other, a running log of their affair—flirtation, wordplay, dirty talk. Two or three times they'd gotten into "fights," but it had never felt serious. It had always felt like play-fighting. Now he realized that the whole thing had been play for her.

He put the phone in his pocket and sat feeling empty.

Hannah emerged from the house, also wearing jeans and a t-shirt, and helped him bag the leaves. They worked well together. Inside, they made love, in a perfunctory way, for the first time since he confessed. Hannah closed her eyes, the two lines between her eyebrows deepening. He wasn't sure that he could do it at first, but the mechanics of the act took over. Afterwards they lay together like they hadn't for years.

There was no question about it: despite everything, he still loved Hannah, in a way. And apparently she still loved him. Was willing to allow him back into their life. Maybe there was a way to come back from this, to reassert control over his life, to piece things back together again. To be forgiven.

Maybe.

Sometimes the young men ignored him and sometimes they remembered he was there and one of them would come over and poke him, shove his head, or laugh at him.

"Hey, you stupid motherfucker."

"You stupid rich motherfucker."

"You think you're special?"

"Fuck you."

"Fuck you, man."

"You're nothing."

"You are nothing, motherfucker."

"You got this big fucking house, but you ain't nothing."

His lack of reaction disappointed them. He had retreated inside himself, was holing up. Remembering pieces of his life without trying to make sense of them. His own youth. He might have but had never done anything quite like this. There had been drugs, danger, music—punk, hardcore—sex. After his brothers were away at college he'd brought friends to the island. In the morning, they would be laid out on the lawn like casualties of war.

He knew that, in one way or another, this would have to end, knew that in so many ways he deserved this.

"What are we going to do with him?" one of them said. They shrugged. No one was the leader. No one wanted to take charge. They had no plan.

He watched Priya get into her car and drive off. She was dressed in black boots and a polka dot dress, ready for another day in the classroom. He sat for a while longer. He could follow her to school, forget all about this. Let this flirtation with danger, or whatever it was, die out. Instead, he got out of the car and walked across the street toward the converted factory building. He was not, he *was* going to do this. He was doing this. He was hyper-aware of everyone in the area. An old woman wearing a red wool jacket walking a small white dog. An old man wearing a cap. A younger couple with tattooed forearms. He felt the Sig Sauer secured against the small of his back. Shooting the gun had become automatic for him—double action pull followed by single action, or double action pull followed by a de-cock.

The lobby was empty. He waited for the elevator. Inside the elevator, he put on the blue gloves he'd taken from a science lab at school. He already knew there were no cameras in the elevator or hallways. It was all easy.

The apartment door was not locked. A sign. He'd been prepared to force the door open with his credit card, but now he didn't have to. Clearly a sign. He turned the handle slowly, entered the apartment, closed the door behind him, the click of the latch nearly silent. Every breath deep and even. A new odor was now layered atop the old odors—him, the new man. There was still the mélange of Priya's body wash and cardamom, but added to that was the faint metallic scent of another man's sweat. Stephen remembered the times he'd spent here. Hours. Entire afternoons. They'd talked about everything. They had climbed inside each other and looked around, as if he'd finally found the person who understood him.

The blinds in the living room were half open, light falling in a slant onto the golden hardwood floors. Everything was still, real but not real. Too real. Unreal.

He removed the gun from the small of his back and held it the way TV cops held their guns, arms extended, feeling removed. This was not him. He was not doing this. Behind or beneath his face things churned; he would not allow those things to surface. Wouldn't feel what he was feeling. It was all about action now.

The man was sprawled in bed on his stomach, half the covers kicked off. His back was muscled and his hair was mussed and he grunted and turned over.

It felt as if he'd done this already. He gave himself no time to think, just shoved the pillow over the man's face, pressed the barrel of the gun into the pillow, let all of his energy concentrate in his finger, which crooked, pulling the trigger. A sudden *pop*. Under the pillow, after a few seconds, red seeped up. He de-cocked the Sig Sauer, the reverberation of the gun's pop loud in his ear—and final. The man's body had gone still, lifeless, emptied.

He had done it.

It had been easy.

There was a stillness to the apartment now, a new, almost beautiful sense of loss. An ending. The clawing things behind his face threatened to break through, but still he wouldn't let them. Priya would feel the stillness the second she entered the apartment. She would freak out, then she would mourn for the man, but then… then, maybe she would come back to Stephen. Did he really believe that?

Something tried to coalesce behind his eyes. He considered hiding in the closet and waiting for Priya to return, though he knew that would be many hours from now. He was not confused because he was not really thinking. He imagined shooting her, too. Pressing the gun to her temple, looking at her beautiful face as it was ripped apart. Imagined shooting himself, too. If he shot her, he would have to shoot himself. A triple murder-suicide that would be reported on the news, their faces in snapshots, then forgotten. Their colleagues and students would talk about them for a long time.

Realizing he hadn't breathed in a while, Stephen took in as much air as he could. He felt scatterbrained. Like he had to remember something.

He found the man's wallet in the jeans left on the floor like a discarded skin. His driver's license. Brian Sanderson. A normal, boring name for a normal, boring man. He shoved the wallet in his back pocket. In the kitchen he took a glass, filled it with water, drank it as he walked out of the apartment.

No one was in the hallway, so he assumed no one had heard the shot. If they had, they must have thought it was something else, or from somewhere else. It could not be coming from inside the luxury apartment building. Gunshots did not happen here. Everything was safe here. They were delusional. He rode down the elevator with the glass still in his gloved hand. Then he walked through the lobby.

Sodden with drink, the boys grew morose. They'd dragged two Adirondack chairs inside the house and sat around the fire with the lights off, flames reflecting off their faces. Stephen couldn't hear what they were talking about, but he heard the names of women, the blunt edge of curse words. *Fuck* and *cocksucker* and *motherfucker* and *cunt* and *fuck* again. They were not much older than his students. He was no longer a teacher; he had left that world behind. He resisted connections between then and now. These men were in their early twenties, if he had to guess. Despite what they had done and were doing to him, Stephen felt sorry for them. They were just lost boys. He was less concerned about what they would do to him than he would have expected.

Let it come, he thought.

He pissed himself, the urine warm and comforting at first, then quickly cold. A day came and went, his abductors out of the house most of the day. Time dripped past. They returned to drink and eat more of his food and laugh and poke his head with stiff fingers. Stephen's lips were chapped. He was thirsty but not hungry. If this was penance, he would endure it. He would endure it anyway. It was not penance.

The tallest of the young men approached, swinging his arms as he walked, the Sig Sauer in his hand. Stephen felt a subsonic fear, the beating of his heart sounding like someone else's.

It was obvious what the young man was going to do long before he did it: a swinging right hook to Stephen's head, the butt of the pistol against his temple. He felt himself fall, his arms struggling to break his fall, the floor rising up to meet him. And then he was out.

Hannah looked up when Stephen walked into the townhouse, after he'd shot another man point blank in the head, a fact he had not even begun to accommodate. It was not real. It couldn't be. She sat at the kitchen table, reading the newspaper, eating a bowl of yogurt and granola. She'd slept late. The night before she'd gone out for a girls' night with colleagues from the real estate office. He had no idea how late she'd returned. He'd been asleep when she got back, and she'd been asleep when he got up.

She looked at his face then quickly away, shaking the newspaper when he scurried past. If he looked different to her, if she could see the mark of what he'd just done on his face, she didn't acknowledge it. Didn't ask him what he was doing home when he should have been at school. Maybe she was afraid of what he would say if she asked.

He was aware of her downstairs as he shoved clothes into an old army duffle bag. Knowing where he was going already, and thinking optimistically, he needed all his cold weather clothes. Flannels and thermals. He packed his running shoes, his hiking boots, a pile of books that had been on his bedside table forever. He was not thinking clearly, but he knew he was going to the island. It was a safe place in his mind, the past. He pictured it as a safe haven, as if he could pull the shadows of the trees around himself. He felt like he was forgetting something.

He found a pad of paper and a pen on her bedside table and scrawled a quick note. *I'm sorry, I can't do this anymore. Stephen.*

Hannah did not look up at him as he walked back through the kitchen. He closed the door behind him, looked back briefly at the townhouse.

He walked down the street, the weight of the bag across his shoulder, the Sig Sauer against his back, wondering how much time he had. It all depended on what Priya was doing that day, how long she was away from the apartment, whether she had her after-school science club. Maybe someone else had discovered the body already. Maybe someone had called 911.

He rented a car and drove up 93, never more than five miles over the speed limit, glancing at the fall foliage on either side of the highway. It was strange how normal everything felt. There were some leaf peepers around—old men and women driving Lincolns and Oldsmobiles—though it was past peak.

He felt more alive than he had in years. More completely *himself*. In one way he had transcended who he had been before, reached a higher level of being. In another way he was operating in survival mode. He wondered if this was how it always felt to kill. He could understand how that feeling could become addictive.

He figured he had a week, max, before they found him and he was made to pay for what he'd done. He didn't actually expect to winter on the island, but he had to have a plan. The island was his plan.

It was early morning at the lake house, the world outside purple. Stephen had been untied. A small mercy. He lifted himself from the floor and rubbed his numb arms. It took several minutes to get feeling back into the muscles, and he wondered if he would have lost feeling for good if they'd left him tied up, if he would have been paralyzed, marked by this incident forever. His entire body ached from sleeping on the floor—if being sprawled unconscious could be called sleeping. He righted the chair, stepped out of the shadows under the loft, stretched.

The lake came back to life in a series of grays and blues. He was hungry and sore. He had pissed himself again in the night. The cold kept the smell from being too pungent; he shook against it. He did not feel ashamed by the workings of the body, just annoyed.

The house had been ransacked, his things scattered, books with pages torn out, his clothes crumpled. Worst of all, his Sig Sauer had been taken. He felt exposed and vulnerable without the gun. He didn't think they would come back and shoot him, but he had no way to protect himself now. Words had been smeared onto the walls with what he assumed was shit at first, before realizing it was dried hot chocolate. Fuck the Rich. Eat the Rich. An anarchy symbol in what looked like blood but was probably ketchup, someone's handprint in red. Vomit flecked a pile of clothes. They had torn the doors off cabinets, smashed the sink, leaving the faucet hanging like a broken bone, flour coating everything. His bag of rice had been burst open and scattered like seed. One of them had left an absurdly neat turd by the sliding glass doors, a turd that looked animal but was clearly human.

Despite the destruction, the vandals had left the windows intact, had not destroyed the firepit or anything in the bathroom, had not wrecked anything he needed to keep himself alive on the island. Another small mercy.

After picking out the guitar strings, he built a fire from embers reluctant to come back to life, rubbed his hands, walked into the bathroom. He had to wait almost two minutes before the water heated up, then he peeled off his old crusted clothes and stepped inside the stream, waiting for the water to run clear off of him. He scrubbed the dry itchy skin under his beard, rubbed his armpits and crotch and asshole. He felt strangely alive, as if he had defeated the young men, when all he'd done was survive them. He felt like he understood them, even appreciated them. They could have done far worse. They could have violated him. They could have beaten him, broken bones and ribs. They could have shot him. His head still hurt, but he was not injured. He would carry what they had done to him for the rest of his life.

He dressed in jeans, a thermal shirt and a flannel. As he cleaned, he warmed and took off the flannel. He cleaned clothes in the bathtub and hung them up to dry. He picked up an intact can of beef stew from the floor, cooked and ate it, the food almost flavorless, mucky brown and white chunks. It felt good to eat. He imagined music in the house, but aside from the sound of himself, the house was silent.

It Never Snows in Vietnam

Luke was into Ka-Bars and Kalashnikovs. Semi and fully automatic rifles. Shurikens. MAC-10s. He was into brass knuckles and hollow point bullets. He had subscriptions for *Soldier of Fortune* and *Guns & Ammo* and he pored over every issue, sometimes bringing them to school in his military backpack to show his two friends, Tommy and Mark, who were kind of into it, but not into it the way he was. He couldn't help himself. He rattled off calibers and bore sizes and talked about the latest model coming out from Smith & Wesson, Uzi, Sturm Ruger. He liked to debate 9mm vs. .45, though he had no one to debate with. He was a 9mm man when he was in seventh grade, more into the .45 in eighth. His uncle had a .45. They would shoot together in his uncle's backyard.

Luke lived with his grandparents and his mother in the garden center his grandparents owned and ran. When he went into sixth grade, he was able to convince his mother to let him move into an outbuilding behind the house. He taped posters on the walls: movie posters from *Terminator* and *Red Dawn*, a calendar full of beer models his uncle had given him, photospreads of guns he'd ripped out of his magazines. His mother wouldn't let him own a gun, but he kept a collection of brass knuckles, knives, shurikens, and ammo she didn't know about in a footlocker underneath his bed. Most of them he bought at the flea market out by 28. He liked to shop at army surplus stores. His uncle would take him.

In the dead of night, Luke liked to venture into the woods surrounding the garden center. He'd take his largest hunting knife, in a sheath around his leg, and slide his brass knuckles in his pocket. He wore camouflage pants and an olive-green t-shirt. It wasn't play, he wasn't a little kid. He thought about his father in Vietnam while he stalked the woods. His father was MIA, could still be on the run over there. Hiding in the tunnel systems or holed up in the jungle. Surviving maybe alone, maybe with another MIA or two. Maybe he was a POW, but Luke liked to imagine him surviving alone, killing only when he had to.

The woods went on for miles. He could travel them up out of the town, into the White Mountains if he wanted to. Sometimes he disturbed night animals. He was sure there were lynx out here, but he only ever saw bobcats and raccoons, once or twice a fisher cat, not animals to be trifled with. He used face paint he ordered from the back of *Soldier of Fortune* to make himself invisible. If his mother ever caught him, she'd lose her shit. It was easy to sneak out of the outbuilding, along the back of the farmhouse where his mother and grandparents slept, out into the woods.

If the moon was full, he could throw his shurikens, aiming at a thick pine near the edge of a field. He liked the sound the shuriken made when it stuck in the meat of the tree. A sound like deadly silence. He liked to imagine sticking the blade of the knife into the belly of the enemy, following through and bringing the fucker up off his feet. He always pictured the enemy as Vietnamese, though now there were Iranians to worry about too. Russians. In five years he could join the military. He planned to become a Navy SEAL. Kill whatever enemy they faced then. There were always enemies.

When there was no moon, he would hunker and slither through the woods, working on his woodscraft, practicing silence. Letting his instincts take over. Once, he saw the largest owl swoop down onto the field to take something shrieking in its claws. Once, he saw a young moose, more than six feet tall but thin, walking down the center of a trail, staggering a little, probably sick.

The next morning, if it were a school day, he'd be tired, but no one would notice, not his grandparents, not his mother, not his teachers. He'd eat the breakfast his grandmother made, shove his magazines into his backpack, head out for the bus stop. He hated school. Everyone he knew hated school, but not as much as him. It was a waste of his time. He already knew more than most of his teachers about the things he cared about, and the other things he didn't care to learn. He already had a life plan.

His uncle Jimmy picked him up one Friday after school. It was late in the year to go camping, October, but his uncle brought cold weather gear, zero-degree sleeping bags, a good canvas tent. They drove up 93 without talking, his uncle lighting a cigarette every half hour or so, Luke trying not to look at him. His uncle looked more and more like his father in the only picture he had of him. His hair was short and he was tall and handsome, like the lead on a TV show. Unfortunately, Luke had got his mother's height (short) and half the features of his father's face and half his mother's. His face was too thin, his eyes too small, but Uncle Jimmy was handsome. Sometimes he had girls with him, but not this time. This time it was just Jimmy and Luke.

There were plenty of sites at the campground off the Kancamagus to pick from, and Jimmy picked one with easy access to the river. He reversed the pickup into the site and they set up camp, Jimmy drinking Budweiser out of a cooler. He gave one to Luke, who tried to hide the fact that the taste made him sick. When Jimmy wasn't looking he dumped it in the woods, the foam swallowed by duff.

It was dark by the time they had everything set up and were rummaging the woods for firewood. Luke didn't know what he was looking for, but he brought back branches and twigs and a large fallen limb that made Jimmy laugh.

"That's right, bonfire motherfucker." He smiled and ruffled Luke's hair, which made him feel good and bad at the same time. He was no little kid.

They built the fire in stages. The kindling and a pyramid of small branches, then the larger branches, finally the limbs they'd started collecting after Luke brought back the first one.

Jimmy was drunk. Luke could tell because his eyes shone in the fire and he talked more than usual.

"Your father took me up here once. He was probably sixteen, I was probably fourteen. We got wasted, boy, I'll tell you. Absolutely *wrecked*. Usually there were a dozen of us up here on Tripoli Road, getting fucked up, partying, girls, all that. But one time it was just me and him. We got fucked up and we wrestled. He was always stronger than me, but I wasn't afraid to fight dirty. You learn to fight yet?" He seemed to suddenly remember Luke was there.

"I've been in some fights."

"Yeah? How'd they go?"

"I mean… I won 'em."

Jimmy nodded and smiled. In the firelight his grin seemed evil, like some horror movie villain.

"That's right. You're a Volpe alright. Have another beer."

"Nah."

"Suit yourself."

Luke fell asleep in the lawn chair. The next thing he knew his uncle was shaking him awake.

"Get in the tent and sleep. It's more comfortable in there."

He nodded, groggy, moved into the tent, folded into the sleeping bag, but then he couldn't sleep. Listened to the sounds the woods made all around him. Thought he heard bears moving through the undergrowth, but maybe that was just Jimmy. He wondered what his father heard every night. There were different animals in Vietnam, different plants, but the same stars in the sky.

It got cold at night, and he heard rain pattering on the canvas tent and his uncle snoring. When he opened his eyes, he could barely see Jimmy's face. It was easy to imagine it wasn't Jimmy.

The rain still pattered in the morning, but they were able to stoke the fire back to life and cook a can of beans on it. They ate with a spoon straight out of the can. Luke felt tired, like something washed up on shore. They walked down to the river. By the middle of the morning the sun was out. It was cold but got warmer quickly. They walked the river, stepping from stone to stone.

His uncle taught him how to tie flies and how to take a brook trout off a line without snagging himself. He taught him how to fillet the fish with a hunting knife, how to cook it on the military cookset. He'd been in Vietnam, too, but only for four months before the evacuation. He'd been there when the helicopters left Saigon. He'd been lucky. They ate the fish without talking. Luke wanted to ask what his father was like as a kid but didn't want to sound dumb.

"You got a girlfriend?" Jimmy asked him.

"Nah."

"Why the hell not? You're a good-looking kid. Get yourself a girlfriend, Luke. Treat her right. Listen to her. That's the trick. It's a simple trick, but you'd be surprised how many people don't seem to know it. Listen to a woman and she'll do almost anything for you."

Luke tried to smile. Girls at school thought he was a freak.

"Can we shoot your .45?"

"Sure, we can shoot the .45. Why the hell not?" He felt his uncle looking at him, looking at his camouflage pants, the gray sweatshirt he wore. He could smell the sweat on himself. He felt small.

When they got back from the camping trip his mother was in the kitchen with someone he'd never seen before. He was probably as tall as Jimmy but broader, with a square face. He smiled at Luke.

"This is Mike, honey," his mother said.

He nodded and felt out of place. Smelled like sweat and woodsmoke. He felt like there was dirt all over his face. His first instinct was to take his hunting knife out and gut the man right there at the kitchen table. He imagined his intestines falling out.

"Hey, buddy," Mike said. "Your mother's told me a lot about you."

Luke couldn't stop nodding. He wanted to say something, something to hurt the man or hurt his mother or hurt both of them but didn't feel smart enough. He left and got some clothes to change into, took a long hot shower. A shower had never felt so good.

The man was still sitting with his mother at the kitchen table when he walked through again. They leaned toward each other.

Jimmy picked him up from school every week. They would go hiking locally or go up to the White Mountains. Once, on an Indian summer day, Jimmy showed up on a softail Harley. His mother and Mike sat at the kitchen table after breakfast.

Mike wore an undershirt and pajama pants. Luke was not used to him yet, didn't plan on ever getting used to him.

"You're not taking him anywhere on that thing," his mother said. She was small, like him, with a thin face full of freckles. He used to think she was the prettiest woman in the world, but now he wasn't so sure. She worked at the garden center.

Jimmy looked at her, looked at Luke.

"You coming?" he said, handing Luke a helmet. Luke put it on. He felt like he was flying as his uncle took the backroads, fast, leaning into the curves. He ceded control to his uncle and to the motorcycle. It felt good.

When they got back, his mother and Mike were watching a movie in the back room and his grandparents were out talking to people at the garden center. He went out to help them.

He figured he could hire someone to kill Mike, or he could do the job himself. He wanted the satisfaction of doing it himself. He would have to figure out a way to do it so his mother never suspected him, so Mike disappeared forever. Or maybe he could poison him so it looked like an accident, so his mother knew he was gone.

There were more than 2,000 MIAs. Most were probably dead, but some could still be alive, either held as POWs or surviving, somehow, in that hostile country. Luke was sure his father was alive somewhere. He would have known if his father was dead. He had never felt as angry at anyone as he was at his mother for not feeling the same way. Sometimes she would look at him as if she wanted to explain something to him, but she never did.

His grandfather was the one who tried to explain it to him.

"I know you're angry," he said, which felt good. At least someone admitted it. "But your mother has a right to live her life. Doesn't she seem happier since Mike's been around?" She did, but Luke wasn't going to admit that. His grandfather was his mother's father. Of course he was going to side with her.

Luke brought the brass knuckles into school, and one recess he wore them when he walked over to two of the kids who'd been making fun of him for years. They called him Rambo. Mocked him. One of the kids' faces was like raw meat when they pulled him off. The other kid had run away.

He worked at the garden center on the three days he was suspended. It felt good not to be at school. The season would be over as soon as Halloween passed. Now they sold pumpkins that came in by the truckload. Little kids ran all over the place, picking apples. There were pies, the smell of wood burning.

When he asked his uncle if he'd ever killed anyone in 'Nam, Jimmy looked at him for a long second.

"Don't ever ask anyone that," he said.

They sat for a while in Jimmy's backyard. One of Jimmy's girlfriends was in the house behind them. She seemed about three years older than Luke, but she was probably older. She wore a t-shirt and nothing else, and her eyes were spooky.

"I don't know how many I killed over there, but, yeah, I killed someone. You fire into the jungle mostly. Who knows how many you killed. I only know for sure I killed one, this little gook climbing over the fence, trying to get away. He might have been about your age. Younger. Who knows. He was the only one I took aim at and shot. I remember the way his hand came free from the fence, his back twitching backwards. When he was on the ground I shot him in the face."

He didn't have to say it: Luke could tell he regretted it, wished he'd never done it.

"You do what you have to do."

Luke nodded.

His mother's bedroom was on one side of the farmhouse, his grandparents' on the other. He could see their bedside lamps when they were on. When they were off, it was safe to go out into the woods.

He bought a night vision sight, and one night he climbed a tree on the edge of the forest and looked through it into his mother's bedroom. It took him a while, but he was able to sight in on Mike. They were in bed together but not doing what he was afraid they'd been doing. Mike wore no shirt. His hair was messy. He was leaning on one elbow and smiling at his mother. If he had a sniper rifle, he could have, and would have, taken the shot.

He found out where Mike lived—across town in an apartment complex. It took him an hour to walk there. It was across the street from a shopping plaza. A Market Basket. A Dick's Sporting Goods. Kids played in the apartment complex parking lot. They looked at him but didn't say anything.

He walked back, at first down busy streets and then past neighborhoods. Finally he was back in the woods.

Mike took him to see Rambo: First Blood Part II at the local cineplex. Mike wore a button-up red shirt and green pants. While they sat together in the theater, Luke could feel the man beside him cringe anytime there was violence on screen. Luke had a hard time following the plot but couldn't help thinking of his father throughout the entire thing. His father was Rambo, and his father was one of the MIAs Rambo was sent to document the existence of, but not to rescue. He got lost in the movie and forgot he was sitting next to his mother's boyfriend, that just by being here he was betraying his father.

He brought his knife to school. He wasn't sure he was going to use it at first. He just wanted to show it to Tommy and Mark. They looked at it, looked at him, scared. Over the past few weeks they'd stopped talking to him unless he talked to them first. They'd started playing D&D in the library during recess. He had no interest in dragons and elves. He talked about buying a Beretta and shooting his mother's new boyfriend in the face. Most of the time he was alone.

He got in another fight, this time pounding his tormentor with his bare fists. At the end, he thought about pulling his knife out, but he was pulled off the kid first. The fights earned him respect from the worst kids who hung out in one corner of the parking lot. They taught him how to smoke cigarettes. At first it made him lightheaded, but then he got used to it.

Once the season was over, his grandparents had less to do around the garden center. His grandfather went over the books. His grandmother canned and cooked and crocheted. They would watch the Pats every Sunday, sometimes just him and his grandfather, sometimes with Jimmy. And now sometimes with Mike, too. Luke didn't care about football but knew his father had, so he tried.

When the first snow fell, he went out after dinner and walked as far as he'd ever walked in the woods. He'd thought he could go up to the White Mountains, but he reached a dead end, a section of churned up land. Felled saplings pushed together. They were going to build something here—a new mall, maybe. He watched the snow slowly accumulate. It never snowed in Vietnam.

Mike took him to a firing range. He was surprised but acted like he wasn't. Mike let him shoot his 9mm. It felt different than Jimmy's .45. He thought about turning the gun on Mike right there in the firing range but didn't want to put his mother through that.

When he got into his third fight, he had a tire iron one of his new friends had given him. He broke the other kid's arm, a satisfying crack he could feel all the way through his own arm. After that, they talked about sending him away to an alternative school. They called him incorrigible. He knew the vice principal was afraid of what he might do. He cited work Luke had done in his English class, journal entries that were supposed to be private, which mentioned plans to murder someone called M.

His mother seemed devastated. Broken by it. She'd tried hard to raise him right, all by herself.

When the time came to go to another school, he put on the jeans his mother had bought him instead of the camouflage pants he always wore. He put on a black t-shirt with a band he'd started listening to, Megadeth. He slid the brass knuckles in his back pocket. His mother looked at him. He was changing; she could tell. It was too early to tell if it was for the better or not, but she decided to believe it was. He let her.

Redacted Records

Larry doubted the man had any money. This kind of operation, a used record store? Money was not the point. It was the kind of thing a man spent his life saving for, scrimping and struggling at some factory gig so he could spend his golden years in a musty old shithole full of moldy records because he loved music. The place on River Road was big and well organized and music was blaring out of old stereo speakers, some kind of jazz fusion with a lot of jagged guitar in it, and the man, Joe Lucie, was obviously living his best life, a big old cigar, unlit, stuck in his mug, smiling down at his granddaughter (Larry assumed) who ran around the place wreaking havoc. The snow out the window was wet and wild, the first day of the New Year. He hated to do what he was being paid to do, but a job was a job and he wasn't about to get particular about it, not at his age. He'd been doing this for almost fifty years at this point, an unbelievably long run of good luck, had spent only six months in the slammer once, on a B&E conviction. He was not one to question providence. Joe Lucie was living his best life, sure, but so was Larry Parrish.

Larry browsed the R&B and soul—reading or pretending to read some of the liner notes, trying to fit in, look like some big music connoisseur. It was easy: any old white guy could fit that bill. The granddaughter was probably four years old, maybe five, maybe ten, what the hell did he know from kids, and she was running amok around the place hiding under the shelving units. Her hair was all mussed up and she wore a striped shirt and her cheeks were red from all the running around she was doing, and even Larry, who didn't know from kids, knew she would crash out soon and sleep the sleep of the dead. Naptime. All he had to do was wait for that moment and then he could take Joe aside, maybe walk him around to the back of the building (he'd think of some reason to get him back there), where they could see the dirty Merrimack River swallowing up some dirty snow, and put a bullet in his skull. Simple as that. Happy New Year.

Larry Parrish never wondered what anyone he offed had done to deserve what they were getting. That was above his paygrade. He left that to Santayana and to God. Let them deal with it, sort the guilty from the innocent, etc. He thought of himself as an old school executioner, like something out of the Middle Ages, had always fashioned himself that way, a needed member of society, someone that kept the cogs of society running by doing the things no one else wanted to do. A kind of garbage man. Maybe he would pay for it in the afterworld, but he would worry about that then.

He never wondered, usually, but now he did, for just a split second, imagining Joe Lucie going in a little too deep on a gambling habit he'd been fighting his whole life, the ponies maybe, he could picture Lucie on the tarmac out at Rockingham poring over a racing sheet, smoking one of those cheap stogies that was now stuck in his face like an affectation but was actually a prop to help him get over that other habit. It was too bad.

The little kid, what was she, six, seven years old, was playing with the pleats of his pants, and when he looked down at her she shuffled away like a sprite, playing her little game. He smiled a grizzled smile at her, then looked over and saw Joe Lucie looking straight at him, a twinkle in his eye, but like he knew what was about to come. Like he forgave Larry in advance.

Artifacts of the Civil War

Afterwards, they returned to the motel room, where Antonio dug the 8-ball out of the front pocket of his too-tight jeans, slit open the plastic bag with his Swiss army knife, and emptied some blow onto the particle board dresser, the TV's matte black screen reflecting the scene back in crooked silhouettes. While Lorene showered—steam and her bad singing, some half-recognized song from the 80's, something about luft balloons, drifting from the half-open door—Antonio laid immaculate lines out on the dresser top. The grain of the dresser's plastic surface was absurd. No wood in the history of the world had ever looked like that.

He wanted to wait for Lorene but couldn't, snorting two lines before she emerged from the bathroom, hunched forward on the chair made of the same material as the desk, with a dark brown cushion. The big mirror at the end of the room fogged up. At the edge of the light's reach, on the carpet, was the bloodstain Antonio had noticed when he first walked in but hadn't told Lorene about, knowing she'd get spooked. She was superstitious, believed in even the stupidest shit. Now he walked over and knelt down, touching the bloodstain with his fingertips. Impossible to tell if it was from years back or last week.

Finally Lorene slid out of the bathroom, white towel wrapped around her body barely covering her, the fat of her arms and thighs and breasts slopping out, hair like snakes. She pushed Antonio away when he tried to grab her, pull open the towel, let all her treasures fall out. She laughed and said, "Fuck you, Antonio. Let me have a line first, for Christ's sake."

In the mirror, he watched her bend over, hold the rolled twenty to her nostril, snort the coke then stand up straight, almost tipping over backwards, and he watched himself watching her, as if he were the ghost of someone else. Wearing skinny jeans and a black t-shirt so old and worn it was gray, his skin ashy. He was not brown or black but gray and his eyes were green and he was skinny as fuck, and all he wanted to do was consume this woman in front of him, eat her up, throw her onto the bed and fuck her, but she was eyeing him now and laughing, folding her legs up under her in a way he didn't think was possible, considering her bulk, on the bed.

"What are you *looking* at, 'Tonio?"

"I'm looking at *you*. You're fucking gorgeous."

"Oh, fuck you."

He bumped another line. Distant music played inside his head, beats made from older beats, like antique music, which made sense because they'd spent the night wandering the old battleground for hours before finally finding the artifact.

"Let's fuck," he said.

"Okay, sure, let's fuck. Come fuck me, big boy."

Underneath the towel she was moist and clean and he smelled between her folds and ate her out, then threw his clothes off. She was loud, urging him on. His heart beat hard, and he brought her at least, *at least*, to the edge—he could never tell if he brought her over, women a forever mystery—two times, turning her over, and even though she was big she was athletic, grinding on his joint until he got his nut off inside her and she lay there all white and pasty and wasted, her breath coming hard and fast. Antonio could hear his heart in his chest, lolloping.

"Was that what you wanted? Huh?"

"That was what I wanted, baby. That was exactly it."

They'd been together two months, and it was still this good. Which made him wonder. How long could something like this last? In his experience, not much longer. He'd met Lorene in a bus station outside Philly, where she'd been hunched over in a harsh spitting wind wearing only a too-big black hoodie and dirty jeans. She'd asked him if he was holding—it didn't matter *what*. He hadn't taken advantage of her the way some guys would, had allowed her to become a person to him before he fucked her. She was not the first white girl he'd fucked but the first one who stuck around afterwards.

Since there was no alarm clock in the motel room, he checked his cell phone: 2:47. Not that it mattered. Time relative. Turning on the TV, he found *Scarface,* and they kind of watched that, kind of just sat there, honey-eyed, Lorene leaning forward, naked, as if her body didn't mean anything now, as if she didn't care if he saw it anymore. They had passed beyond the sexual part of the night, and also past the criminal adventure part, and were now settled in. Maybe they would fuck again, but not for another two, three hours. Antonio wasn't sure what to talk about with Lorene, they were still so new. She had already told him all about her family, abusive father, out-of-it mother, how she'd escaped from them and was never going back. They had agreed not to talk about their pasts again, which was fine with Antonio.

Nine o'clock the night before, they'd been eating inside a McDonald's, downtown Gettysburg. He ate a Big Mac, she ate two Quarter Pounders, and they looked around them, casing everything. There were a few older people and some local kids. A Black kid behind the counter worked the fry-o-lator, but everyone else was white. An old woman whose face resembled pink plastic wore a poncho. A local cop came in, bought a coffee, joked with a middle-aged woman who might have been the manager, walked out again. No one paid any attention to them, so they were able to tell themselves they didn't really exist here. They were travelers from another time period, on a mission. His buddy Danny had told him it would be an easy haul.

When they walked out of the McDonald's it was deep night, easy to slip into the battlefields around town; they were right there, the town built up on top of them. The night was cooling. He could feel Lorene beside him, her breath deep and even, trying to calm herself, telling herself that there were no ghosts out here, when, if there were ghosts, they sure as fuck would be walking the battlefields with them. They headed toward the valley just down from Little Round Top, where they'd stood a few hours previously with dozens of tourists looking out at the battlefield where most of the carnage had taken place. During the day women on horseback led tours, and there was an old dude dressed like a Union soldier, another like a Confederate officer, telling the same story in different ways.

Everything had paled in the night. The earth seemed to breathe beneath them. Small, empty roads crisscrossed the battlefields, and there were memorial sculptures everywhere, obelisks and soldier statues indistinguishable from one another, limestone seeming to grow out of the ground. Antonio grew weary of walking.

"It's like a place a vampire would live, am I right?" Lorene said.

"Sure, baby."

"*Dawn of the Dead* or something."

Even though they scared the shit out of her, Lorene liked horror flicks. They'd watched all the *Saw* movies together, her body jiggling beside him every time something disgusting happened. Walking out onto a battlefield at night was a big deal for her. She was trying to hold in her fear. Antonio was tempted to startle her, grab her arm and yell something, but he knew she didn't play. Wouldn't forgive him.

He saw a figure in the darkness about ten feet from them, a man, he was pretty sure. He was wearing blue rags and he limped, and when they got closer the man ducked into the woods and ran away. They should have heard him breaking through the brush but didn't. "What the fuck?" Antonio said. He decided to act like he hadn't seen anyone.

It took them a long time to find anything even conceivably worthwhile. They stopped in the battlefield often to dig, with their heels, then with the small metal trowel he'd wedged into the back pocket of his skinny jeans. He'd assumed there'd be bones under the ground anywhere they stopped. He was hoping for a lot more than bones—shells, old uniforms, something tangible he could fence. His buddy Danny claimed to have found a bloodied section of a Confederate uniform and got $300 for it online. The last body had been found here in 1999. *1999.* Of course they were going to find something.

While they rooted around in the ground Antonio felt the spirits of dead men rising up in protest—*let us fucking rest, already*—but didn't say anything to Lorene. He waited to see another figure in the woods, but didn't, so convinced himself he had never seen the first figure. They were near a stand of trees on the edge of what the tour guide called "The Valley of Death" when he dug up the bone, feeling it reverberate against the handle of the trowel. "Holy shit," he heard himself say. First he came to the edge of the jaw, with one rotten molar still clinging to it, then he dug it out. The guy had had bad teeth—most people probably did in the nineteenth century. Lorene acted like it was no big deal, but he could tell she was afraid of it.

Now the jaw rested on the other side of the TV. It had looked pure white in the moonlight but appeared gray in the motel room.

"That thing creeps me out, man," Lorene said, following his gaze.

"He don't mind. You don't mind, do you, Colonel Steubbins?" Antonio had named the jawbone while they were walking back through the battleground. He'd made it talk to Lorene, who wouldn't play along, got all huffy until he reminded her about the coke. He wondered what the hell had happened to her to make her so afraid of everything but wasn't about to ask. If he kept her high, she was always good to him. He wondered what she would do once this thing ended. Couldn't even imagine. She wouldn't go back to her family. Maybe she'd find another man who would take care of her for a while, just keep going through men until her luck ran out. He didn't hold out much hope for her.

"I don't understand who would ever want to buy that thing, though."

"Civil War freaks, that's who, babe. They're out there. You just have to know how to find them. I got connections."

The coin was shoved deep into the front pocket of his jeans, the coin he'd found but for reasons he couldn't explain to himself hadn't shown Lorene, an 1861 half-dollar. On one side of the coin were the words Confederate States of America, on the other a weird picture of Liberty looking sad, the surface worn but in decent shape. Finding it had affected Antonio more than he could have imagined, in a deeply private way. It was like finding an old Nazi uniform or something, something clearly evil, tainted. Somebody who believed in slavery had held that coin in his pale palm, someone who had fought to keep Antonio's ancestors in bondage. Someone who had probably raped his great-great-great grandmother and whipped his great-great-great grandfather. He had never really thought of it that way until that moment; the Civil War seemed so distant and he didn't really have a mind for history, but there it was, in his hand, proof positive. If the asshole who owned the coin had had his way, Antonio would have been born a slave, would still be a slave today. They'd call him a half-breed, a quadroon, and he'd be picking fucking cotton.

"I don't know, 'Tonio."

"Trust me, babe."

"Why would I start now?"

"Come on, babe." When he nudged her, her body jiggled, in a provocative way, and he reached around to grab one of her breasts, thinking maybe he could get it up again, then noticed her staring at the carpet.

"Oh. My. God," she said, not quietly.

"What?"

"Oh my God, there's a fucking bloodstain over there, 'Tonio!" Her voice grew louder with every word.

"It's nothing, babe. Somebody probably just cut themselves shaving, that's all."

"Are you fucking kidding me?" Upset, Lorene's voice became harpy-shrill. This was one of the things Antonio hated about her. Her voice reminded him of his mother, who'd spent most of her life yelling at him, calling him a no-good piece of shit, but who could also turn around and be kind and loving. He needed to slot himself under her arm every few months, back in Baltimore. She had raised him by herself, and at least tried to do a good job. Since she was always working, he'd had to make it on his own. But his mother was right—he *was* a no-good piece of shit. He fucked up everything he tried to do, burned down everything he'd ever built. At this point he didn't expect anything different.

"L, listen, that stain's not big enough to be from, like, a deathwound."

"Yes it fucking is. Fuckin' A, 'Tonio. You saw that. I know you saw that. Why didn't you tell me, you asshole?"

"What does it matter? I knew you'd just freak out."

"You're damn right I'm going to freak out." Her voice was so loud it penetrated the walls of the motel. Antonio pictured the people in the rooms on either side of them pulling pillows down over their ears. "Who knows who's in here with us right now."

"There ain't nobody here but us, babe."

"I'm sorry," she said, to the air, not him. "I'm so sorry. I didn't know you were here."

"Damn," Antonio said. He cut himself another line, using the edge of his credit card, the plastic on plastic clacking loud, everything so loud now. Little sparks of electricity shot off behind his eyes.

"We have to get the fuck out of here. *Now*."

"We can't leave. It's three o'clock in the fucking morning. Just chill, bitch."

"Oh, *fuck*, Antonio."

He was almost able to convince himself that this experience was genuinely traumatic for her. Something, something horrible, must have happened to her to make her this way, but everyone had shit in their past. Everyone had to learn to handle themselves. She got up out of the bed, put on her dirty clothes from the day before, jeans and a t-shirt. He watched her, wondering why he loved her, if he did. Maybe he did. He snorted another line, rubbed his nostrils with the palm of his hand, picked up the jaw.

"Hey," he said, talking the jaw. "Calm down, bitch. Everything's cool." The jaw in his hand had once belonged to a man, a Union or Confederate soldier, impossible to tell which now. Officer or grunt, either one. A white man, probably, but maybe not. A man who'd died because he'd been sent to fight for something. Who'd had some kind of beliefs.

Antonio had beliefs, too. He believed in survival. He was determined to survive this world, however he had to do it. He heard Lorene slam the motel room door as she left, but the car keys were still on the bedside table, so where the fuck was she going? She wasn't going to stand out on the ramp to the highway and hitchhike, and even if she did who was going to pick her up? Some lonely trucker? Yeah, probably.

He snorted another line and waited ten minutes, *Scarface* still playing on the TV, then got up, dressed, followed her, slamming the motel room door behind him, fuck everyone else. The parking lot was well lit, three quarters full, most of the cars shitty, like his, decades-old, though there was a Cadillac Escalade towing a fishing boat. He had an urge to jump on board and slash the covered seats, kick the captain's wheel. The Confederate coin, about the size of a condom, burned in his pocket. It had to be worth something. Something big, he hoped. It could change his life. It wouldn't take much.

The night clerk, a short Black dude with dreads, was still working the desk, watching TV, the glow of the screen turning his face other colors. Even from this distance, Antonio could see Lorene standing near the on ramp to the highway, white shirt glowing as if she were the ghost. He wanted to tell her to come back. He wanted to yell out to her: "Lorene, come on, you know I love you, baby." But what did he know about love? What did he know about anything? He was thirty years old and had no permanent place of residence. No job. No prospects. He was a fuck up. But, hell, at least he lived a full and free life. Give him that much credit.

As he walked slowly toward her, he thought about the motel room behind him. It would be a ghost party now, the jawbone ghost talking with the murdered ghost. He imagined a Black dude, a drug deal gone wrong. They'd be sharing some coke and talking some deep philosophical shit, like what it was like to be dead. The meaning of human existence. If Antonio were still there he would be able to pick up on it, absorb it. Learn. What was Lorene afraid of, anyway?

Learning something new about the world? Everything was unknown, and the only way to live was to dive down into it.

She was jerking her thumb into the empty air when he approached. Orange construction cones all around her, the streetlight blinking on and off, yellow and black, yellow and black. Through the light pollution he couldn't see a single star, only a charcoal sky above them, the air muzzy.

He watched a big semi come barreling toward them down the lane.

"Come on, Lorene. Come back," he shouted above the roar of the truck.

"Fuck you. Fuck you, 'Tonio. You don't love me. You never loved me. If you loved me you'd get me out of that fucking motel room. You'd get me out of every-fucking-thing. You'd save me."

"I want to save you, baby. Let me save you."

"Maybe you want to, but you can't. Can you?"

When the truck passed, driving seventy or eighty miles an hour, the draft pulled them along after it, rippling their clothes. She stared at him with eyes that looked like someone had plucked them out, sucked on them for a while, then put them back in.

"You can't fucking save me. You can't even save yourself."

She turned her back to him.

Within minutes another truck was approaching. Was that light on the edge of the horizon? Was a new day dawning already? Antonio reached out and placed both hands against Lorene's meaty back. He couldn't feel bone, only the solid mass of flesh and fat. Her powerful heft. Just before the truck approached, acting on some buried impulse too powerful to quiet, he pushed as hard as he could. If the world were just, she would have been immovable. Rooted as a tree.

The Resurrection Project

After getting out, he tried to make a new life. He moved to upstate New York and started a resurrection project, something that would bring him back to life. It wasn't going to be easy because he was dead inside. Life had fled from him like a beaten dog. It came back the same way.

He moved into an apartment above a little coffee shop, and he woke to the smell of baked goods. There was someone in bed beside him. A woman, younger but not by much. Maybe she just looked younger because life had been kinder to her. She smelled like blood. They'd stained the sheets. When she turned toward him, he was surprised to see his dead sister for a second, but then her face reconstituted itself and became a stranger's.

"Marnie," she said. "You don't remember my name."

"Glen," he said.

"I remember yours." She was dressed in a black tank top that didn't fit. Her breasts slopped out on either side. Her hips made a little mountain under the covers. When he reached for her: "No," she said. "Gotta go."

And then she was bustling up out of bed, rinsing off in the shower, putting on some jeans and high heels and clattering down the stairs like a horse or two. Damn. He tried to remember where he'd met her. Couldn't. Remembered his sister instead. Then stopped doing that.

The resurrection project involved tools and materials he got from the dump. Salvaged boards, pieces of metal. He built a scale model of a life he had lived before: wife, two kids, two-car garage. It was intricate and faithful. He had learned metalworking inside, but this modeling was a skill he hadn't realized he possessed. His scale model kids were five and seven, perfect. They didn't talk back to him. They didn't refuse to come visit him.

It took months.

In the meantime he got drunk, slept with women who were willing to sleep with him, and worked late shifts at the airport loading luggage into the bellies of metal planes. 737s, 747s. He earned begrudging respect by putting his head down and working, and then he earned suspicion because he wouldn't talk to anyone and worked too hard. In the best moments he forgot where he was. He became a machine, moving things from one place to another.

Late shifts did not mean late mornings. He couldn't sleep past six or six-thirty. Sometimes the smell of baked goods woke him, sometimes the birds.

He smashed the scale model of his former life. He used a hammer, and then he lifted the model and brought it down on the floor. He heard himself screaming, primally, but couldn't stop himself, not even after the neighbors started banging on the walls. The cops came and warned him. He sat on the floor looking at the pieces of his project.

Then he started again.

His sister would not come back. Neither would the two strangers he'd killed in the crash. He's been so drunk he couldn't see anything. He got blackout drunk still but had no car so was only a danger to himself. He woke up one fall morning half in a river. If it had been colder he would have gone hypothermic. As it was he shivered and wandered back through the town he barely knew.

The next scale model was bigger. He bought modeling clay and a wooden armature, and he put back together his son and daughter and ex-wife, all of whom refused to see him anymore. His ex-wife had a restraining order out on him. His kids would do the same if he tried to get in touch with them. He made ¾ models of each one of them, and he sat them in the ratty secondhand furniture in his apartment. His son's nose was too small. His daughter's head had a dent in it. His ex-wife barely looked like a person at all.

He wondered how long he could go on like this.

He woke in someone else's apartment. There was a brick wall. A railroad apartment. The woman was small and very pretty and looked like she did a lot of yoga. She smiled at him as if he'd said something kind and he felt confused and wanted to cry. Then he did. He was three towns away; the Uber ride cost him more than twenty bucks.

At work sometimes he thought about climbing into the luggage compartment and going wherever the planes were going. Spokane or Milwaukee or Austin. Someplace that wasn't here.

Finally it snowed. It was the first snow he'd seen since getting out. It was beautiful. He brought the ¾ scale models down from his apartment and carried them, one at a time, out to the woods. He found a copse where the snow hadn't fallen yet, and he set them up in a circle. Then he sat down with them and shivered in the cold.

Inside, he'd had no choice but to tunnel inside himself. Now he was trying to come out a little at a time. He left the scale models there, and he went into the coffee shop below his apartment. He ordered coffee and a lemon cake and he sat at a table watching people.

San Juan

Every time he walked down the rickety wooden stairway, at the spot where he could first see the rocky beach hundreds of feet below, he thought about what it would feel like to fall.

What it would feel like if the walkway gave, wooden planks cracking and sending him hurtling.

What it would feel like if someone were to push him and send him out into space.

He imagined it as a limbo, a time between before and after.

He would pause, feeling vertiginous expectation.

And then one day there was the man standing at the spot, looking down at the beach, and for a moment he was between another before and after.

And then he was doing it.

Bumping into the man, forcing him over the guardrail.

He knew that the endless moment he was experiencing was different than the endless moment the man was experiencing. The man's endless moment would last forever.

The man's body crashed through trees and was hurtling through space hundreds of feet down. He heard the impact of the man's body against rock. He couldn't see him from the bend on the walkway but would once—if—he walked down.

Love as an Act of Revenge (Proof of Concept)

It's about time we got out of this shit. Hit a new high. Swing from the stars. Do something somehow new in the world. Get our heads out of the fucking toilet of consumer culture. That's what the Sailor says, but you can't trust the Sailor. You can't trust anyone, but the Sailor? Forget about it.

—

Alice danced whenever she wanted to dance. She could tear a hole in the floor with her heels. She could howl at the moon with her hips. She could, and often did, make men cry.

—

The archomythopoetics of the American Southwest and West. Old and New.

—

"I ain't had fun like this in years," Jabo said. The pistol on the bench seat of the Buick beside him, the knife still in his hand, flecks of blood dotting the right side of his face and his teeth when he grinned over at her.

—

I killed a man in Juarez, but who hasn't killed a man in Juarez? Or a woman, both.

—

The lines of the electric guitar reached out like the sinuous arms of a many tentacled octopus and swaddled the crowd in its greasy embrace.

—

Maybe we are all fragments of other people, shards sparking off each other. Maybe we are all bullshit, and maybe we are all bullshit detectors. Alice could do almost nothing but dance, in the minds of some men, but Alice in fact could do almost anything, from repairing a motorcycle engine to understanding quantum physics. Doubt was the friction she worked against always, and though sometimes it got old that doubt would never defeat her.

—

There's no mistakes in the world. Everything is meant to be just exactly the way it is. That might surprise some people, but it's the gawldawn truth. You mighta made a mistake, but think about it another way, buddy, and maybe you haven't. Maybe all the cards fell exactly the way they were always fated to.

—

Love can be and is more often than we might expect an act of revenge. A knife blade in a beating heart.

—

Some people learned the hard way not to trust Sailor. Most people never got the chance.

—

The lack of fully realized thematic material is itself thematic material, fully realized. See: the Unfinished Symphony, the epigrammatic stories of Donald Barthelme, the later novels of David Markson. Who is the Christ figure in this Passion play? An argument can be made for any of the characters, aside from Jabo, maybe, more Lucifer than Judas, though also deeply human, aka flawed, fallible, often ugly.

—

Chic(k) in a world of men. Men who sometimes didn't think of themselves as men, as if they had evolved into some higher form of man-woman but who were men all the same. Who wanted to fuck her and tell her how to think about what she was seeing, how to fit it into her conceptual ken, how to kettle it like a fish. Fuck them. She was stronger and smarter than any of them. She had been around a few blocks.

—

It could have been any one of them walking into the old adobe church just across the border, wearing wooden heels that clapped the hardwood floor, a floppy brimmed hat shading eyes already shaded with sunglasses, lips a verdant plum. Any but Sailor, and if Alice the ghost of Alice.

—

Transmutation. Transmutation of words. Transmutation of characters, setting, situations. A mathematical equation. 1,1,1,1. (1+1) (1+1) 4-2. 2. 1, 1. ∞

—

It is the age of the bloated rock star and the overproduced rock record. Easy to forget that real people still exist, but they crawl all over the earth with their small concerns like ants laden with breadcrumbs. They are the kings and queens of their own little concerns.

—

In a map of Mexico from the 1800s, Spanish galleons skirt the borders of a landmass that encompasses what would now be Cali, Texas, and Mexico proper. Everything, *everything*, can be encompassed.

—

The conceit: a ghost town at the edge of what was once liminal land on the edge of the desert but is now sere desert entire. Among the old concrete foundations and the remains of building materials that have petrified in the arid air, one can find scraps of paper, desiccated sometimes to the point of illegibility. At least two different hands are identified, a scrawl that is sometimes drunken sometimes just lazy (Terry Allen's) and another, more mysterious hand. A perfect hand. There is almost, maybe, an authorial voice overlaying everything. Typographical indications (italics, underlining, quotation marks, etc.) do nothing to distinguish one voice from the other.

—

Old Carlotta winds up in a brownstone on the upper East Side, or is it Jamaica? She is 53 but she looks 79, still fine but slightly or more than slightly desiccated. She still has her run of the men. The apartment is crammed with the detritus of several lost lives, hers and others.

—

There is a full-press manhunt out on the Colorado and New Mexico and Kansas and Texas freeways. There is a multiple murderer on the loose. There is a motorsickle chasing down a white line. There is a man and a woman or maybe just a man or hey have you ever considered maybe it's just a woman who dressed like a man and followed all y'all?

—

Sometimes a sentence was all she could squeeze out. It was like shitting out a diamond. But then later she'd look back at it and a diamond it wasn't. Just another piece of shit.

—

Around here you got to watch what you swallow.

—

In the diners and the juke joints and the adobe mom and pop joints and in his own trailer and on the side of the road and in bars and restaurants in Tijuana and LA, he was propped up by a bunch of smoke.

—

There's a power to words that rolls over only the right typography. Beasts of the Western plains.

—

The four of them facing off in that dry Colorado weather, the beauty of it all, the sudden spark of an argument. But before that the four of them dancing drinking and laughing in a way none of them ever had before, comfortable with each other. The great mystery of full-bodied laughter. A fitful connection made.

—

In a way, he could say that everything he'd done he had done it for love. In another way, that was all a load of horseshit.

—

Terry Allen sits at a table in a diner in New Mexico drinking a coffee, looking much the worse for wear, his face all bags. He looks out the window then he looks over at the waitress, a not unpretty woman somewhere in her late thirties/early forties. There is a totting up and a gathering. There is a consideration of all possibilities.

—

Fragmentation in lieu of linear storytelling. A fractured "novel" if by novel we mean epic story. Nevermind length. A transmutation of a concept album from the 1970's. A mythic time in the author's (and, quite possibly, if hypothetically, the reader's) mind. Definitely in the mind of the culture, if there remains an identifiable culture that hangs together in any real way. In the cosmic consciousness of a generation, X. To plumb the depths of *Juarez* is to understand something of the psyche of a forgotten generation. An archeological excavation. Before shit went haywire vis-à-vis so-called technology. A not gentler but a more genuine (?) world.

—

It's the last thing you want to do.

—

There is no end in sight.

—

Alice's heart is plump and red and beats with love for all the world, sometimes. Sometimes it is a deep purple with unending hatred. Alice is no different from any one of us.

—

The very particular and practical nature of the old mexican devil, el viejo diablo mexicano, variable, mutable, and yet somehow always whole.

—

There was always the road running underneath them. Ribbons. Motorsickles or Greymound buses. Cars full of screaming wetbacks wielding knives. Or goodgawd a carload of honest-to-god cheerleaders from the college, all smooth thighs and cocktease who wouldn't give it up for a hundred bucks but would for nothing to someone somewhere else. The road, it got real lonely.

Surely there was more to it than this, a random assemblage of characters stuck in their moments. Surely.

—

Sailor could soliloquize on the state of the world like a motherfucker. Or he could sit there getting drunk with Spanish Alice in a trailer in the Colorado woods and forget about everything. He was a man of many moods.

—

She might as well've been buried under the rubble in that LA earthquake

She might as well've been buried under the rocks in that Colorado avalanche

—

Conceit, continued: gray functionaries fanned out into the sere desert to retrieve scraps of paper on which were written elusive, often epigrammatical words. Words that meant nothing to the gray functionaries, who scanned the scraps of paper with gray eyes and put said scraps into sealed evidence bags to be collated and collected and (most likely) destroyed by some critical central intelligence. Though, predictably, maybe sentimentally but no matter, one of the gray functionaries upon looking at the words written in a hasty maybe drunken hand suddenly felt something beating up through the quagmire of disinterest within him. *Felt* something for the first time in his sad gray life. What would spring from that seed no one could say. Probably nothing good. Nothing easy anyway.

—

No one knew it would come to this.
No one knew it would come to *this*.
No one knew it would come to *this*.

—

You will never believe this thing I have to tell you. Never.

—

Rock 'n' roll as a failed religion in places like LA, Colorado, Tijuana, and Juarez. Chic as the high priestess.

—

The old toddling wooden piano tone. Ivories and rusted strings. The good sex in small rooms, the smaller the room the better, and the better sex in the open air. Young and rough and cruel and crude. And also loving. Whatever the hell that means.

—

There was too much energy when the four of them came together in that tiny spot in Colorado. Something was bound to pop off.

—

There is no sense of an ending in a land in which night doesn't fall for hours or sometimes at all, when the light hangs liminal and dusty and pink and the warmth seeps up out of stone at all hours.

—

Descrying the road home. An open egg shape, death as inevitable end but also return.

—

The (im)possibility of transformation and transmutation personally and (yes) spiritually.

—

In the backrooms of the most famous rock 'n' roll venues of the West Coast, Chic Blundie sat like a verdant goddess. Even the musicians cut their eyes on her jagged beauty. She could write any of them out of existence. And often did.

—

They could be discrete or they could be agglomerated. You take your pick. Depending on your substance of choice and the time of day. The slant of light. In the southwest, the light can hold on to the sky for several days in a row, it sometimes seems.

—

Terry Allen plays piano in an abandoned old hacienda somewhere outside suburban Colorado, somewhere with carpets soaked with floodwaters and the reek of insects breeding. Outside, the wind whips tree limbs around while in the impossibly far distance holy mountains squat as if they're taking a shit.

—

The cataclysms here are only of the natural variety, which is not to say they are not man-made.

—

A heist is predicated on planning. What he done did to that liquor store was straight impulse. He was starting to build a typology of crimes, large and small. Of which he was the sole perpetrator.

—

There is a certain je ne sais quoi involved in shiftings of points of view. An I can become Sailor can become Chic Blundie can become Jabo. That we are all each. A concept that needed no proof.

—

Women come and women go but Chic and Alice were not the kind of women who came and went. They were the kind of women who got their claws into you and didn't let go. And they also did not give a single shit about you. They could float and they could dance and they could do hard arithmetic at night and leave you in the morning. At the end of the epic one of them was dead, while the other might never have existed at all. Where does that leave us? Dangling in the stratosphere, that's where. In the middle of the road facing down an oncoming vehicle, waiting to see if it's a semi or a state fucking cop. Either way, an end is a'coming.

—

The sex was beyond good, beyond description, a whole different level of existence that had her toes curling and some growl in his throat he'd never heard himself make before. They forgot themselves inside it but were well aware that it was only possible exactly in the moment and the place where they were, that it would never happen again in quite the same way, and though she had used her body to earn her living for years by that point this was something entirely different. Neither knew this would number among the last times they would enjoy this particular pleasure.

—

We are all whores, and always have been.

—

The motor inn was a nice place to stop but not a nice place to sleep. Odd odors crawled out of all the corners. More than one person had been killed in room 19. Alice could feel their ghosts, but the ghosts were welcoming. Hungry but not for them. The ghosts simply watched, not at all nostalgic for the ways of the flesh.

—

In the span of one life you can cross only so many borders.

—

He hoarded scattered words written in several different pocket notebooks and on scraps of napkins in diners. Sometimes he'd wipe his face with one of them, his brushy mustache tearing the thin paper, ink smearing his lips blue or black. Other people in some other future days might piece it all together like a lost religious treatise. He wasn't too concerned.

—

From dry country to drier city.

—

It's about time to lose our fucking minds and dive deep into the mire. The mire is where the best stuff can be found, but it never lasts for long. The deepest cuts are always the hardest to heal.

—

I would like to love you, but I don't know how. Who the fuck said that? Some sad and stupid song.

—

The smell of Chic(k) Blundie: eggs and earth, metal, blood, yeast, chocolate and cinnamon. The taste the same.

—

Every story is simple. And there is nothing simpler than a Texas boy.

—

Sometimes he would take his print-outs, his mimeographs, his handwritten notes and he would cut carefully around the words. He would put the words into a sack and toss them around and then he would take them out one by one and lay them all out. It wasn't only William S. Burroughs who did this, his famous cut-up technique. It was a slew of others who believed that words could be magic. Incantatious. Each word following another word making a certain combination that was meant. Meant to be. It was important to start with words imbued with magic already—in his humble opinion it was, at least. Though dead words could be brought to life by proximity. Never discount dead words. Nothing is dead forever.

—

Jabo and the golden needle. He flicks the end of the syringe and sinks the needle into the unblemished flesh of his arm. Out the window: dry chaparral.

—

"Motherfucker, this *is* Paradise."

—

The man with the brush mustache and the crumpled off-brand cowboy hat left a $13 dollar tip on a $5.15 bill.

—

These are not characters, you understand, you have come to understand, but elements of a primal psychology to which we are all prone. And the borderlines are not between countries but between provinces of the call-it-soul. We are *all* fucked in this world of murder and manhunt.

—

Love is always an act. An act of revenge. An act of retribution. An act of the will. An act of negligence. Almost always, if nothing else, an act of desperation.

—

There were pretty people in dire places, or there were dire people in pretty places. That was pretty much the secret.

—

Each drop of rain explodes like a miniature mushroom cloud on the arid earth of the high desert.

—

Jabo is bound to die but not tonight. Tonight he edges deeper into darkness. The dry chaparral. The endless sere.

—

Jabo of the golden mind. Jabo the great unknown.

—

Rock 'n' roll could live without her. She its mythic seer no longer but a woman disappeared in time, going her separate way.

—

Alice wasn't always like this. Before the Sailor took her away from the whorehouse she was just another whore. No. That wasn't true. Not at all. It wasn't true of any of them. Whore is not a true nature but a becoming thing. Like sailor. Or saint. But Alice had been fooled for a time into believing it.

—

And Terry Allen sits in a diner blowing over the brim of another coffee. Looking over the edge at the world out the window through the mirror behind the waitress's head.

—

It's easy to believe in love when that is all that's been fed to you for years. When you have to make do with sad expressions of lust and dry gropings in tiny rooms. It's impossible to believe in love at all, really.

—

Sometimes we dream of breakers rolling in to the coastal shelf.
    Sometimes we dream of rocks.

The Day After Easter

Atlantic City, 2024

Charl could barely move. She wished she could go back to sleep, back to a safe space of weirdness, but she was awake now, in an unsafe space of weirdness, nestled against Don's body, smelling the grody pits of her man, no more grody than her. The Econo Lodge on Madison in Atlantic City. The day after Easter. A cold, steady rain out the window. No one was around this time of morning.

Charl slumped up out of bed, pleasantly shocked to find one last cigarette squirreled away inside the soft pack of Winstons on the table, sitting there in the half-light coming through the open windows. All gray all day. Flattened, a little, but smokable.

And smoke Charl did, stepping out of the motel room onto the walkway looking out onto the back alley and a hotel that didn't exist anymore, boarded up, graffiti-laden. A pile of old clothes heaped in the alley as if someone had dematerialized. A couple stilt-legged seagulls. She shut the door behind her quietly, careful not to lock it. Room 17. A good luck number. Smoke in her lungs good as food in her stomach. Almost. Not really. Not nearly. Her mouth was a cave full of bad smells, reeking of old liquor and stale smoke. The last time she ate? Sometime last night when

Don had found half a pizza in a smashed pizza box. A gift from God. Pepperoni? Definitely pepperoni: she tasted it when she belched.

Don was asleep in the room now. Hopefully.

She went back inside, finished with her first and probably only cigarette of the day (they had no money left) and her precious alone time, spent contemplating the rain's pattern on the alley, the smell of Atlantic City in the morning, something like bacon wafting over from some breakfast place making her feel both hungry and sick, smell of ozone and the cigarette she smoked and the cloud of someone toking some weed nearby, a wake 'n' bake in progress somewhere, trying not to the think about anything in particular, though memories of their last few days together intruded, wild days that ended definitively the night before when he'd barked at her and she'd pushed back at him because she wasn't going to put up with that shit. She was not some fucking towel to use however he wanted. She was, had always been, a fighter. Their first fight: a hallmark of its own.

When she went to shake him in the bed, she knew right away. This was no sleep. No, this was something more serious than sleep. This was death. Heavy as a bear. A little vomit had leaked out the side of Don's mouth, gray and pink from the pizza, stuck in his stubble, and his hair still looked done up, the way he did it up, standing straight up from his forehead—she could still see the striations from the comb—mostly brown but a little gray, too, the fact that he was ten years older than her no longer a thing that mattered. At all. Because he was ... dead. He was not Jesus; he was not going to rise from the dead. It was not Easter; it was the day after Easter.

Alone time was all she would have from now on. That was thought number one. Not worry about him and whatever passed for his soul, as if he had one, but fear for her future. How the hell was she going to get along without Don? I mean, she'd done it for most of her life, so... She'd been with Don only three months, knew in the span of her entire life she would probably barely even remember him and this time she'd had with him, depending on how long she lived herself—a valid question—but he had been everything for those three months. Everything. Her ride-or-die. Her meal ticket. Her supplier. Never mean, until the night before. She'd never even seen him get angry, not at her or anyone else, prior to the night before, but they'd been on a four-day binge without eating or sleeping a whole lot and that could turn anyone mean, so, even though she HAD wished death upon him before she passed out, she'd also understood and fully expected to forgive him in the morning and maybe even, if they both had the energy for it, have some rollicking makeup sex.

They did okay, sexually. At first they'd done it every day, sometimes twice a day, but lately it had been more like every three or four days. She attributed it to his age more than their drinking. They'd gone a week without it, once, and both seemed to forget how to do it, had to approach each other like it was the first time again. Which, considering how early in the relationship it was, worried her. But didn't anymore. There were bigger things to worry about now. She looked at Don's dead face against the pillow. He looked meatier than before, which made no sense, but. Thick brown stubble stuck out of his pale skin like wire that had been pulled through. He always looked better animated. He was an ugly sleeper. Maybe he wasn't dead after all. She stopped herself from checking his pulse, let the possibility of his survival linger. But knew he was dead, definitively.

She assumed he'd choked on his vomit, but it was just within the realm of possibilities that Charl had killed him. Strangled him or put a pillow over his face and pressed as hard as she could. If she wanted to, she could. No question about that. He was not the strongest man she'd ever been with, not by a long shot. She was small but almost definitely stronger than him. What did she remember from the night before, really? Not a whole lot. Him barking, her sulking, her pushing back, him storming out of the motel, him coming back. Not apologizing. Barking again. His face a face she'd never seen before. Not on him. Some scary psycho man face. She'd seen plenty of those. Every woman had.

It was better to remember the time they'd had before they got pissed off at each other. When it had been fun. Easter night. Staggering back onto the boardwalk after those daiquiris at that stupid daiquiri bar, the cop car rolling down the boardwalk real slow, its tires rumbling on the boards, a white cop with a flat head watching them as they staggered against each other, laughing. Karaoke. "Feels Like the First Time." Slot machines all lit up like Easter eggs. The found and providential pizza. The flat endless ocean. The fifth of vodka he'd bought, with what money? They'd kissed sloppy on the beach but were both too drunk to do anything more. It had all been celebratory, revelatory, perfect and fun. Somehow they'd made it back to the Econo Lodge. Obviously. She had no memory of how. And no memory of how the fight started, what it was about. It had been sudden as a chink of light.

Now, here, Don dead, her alone forever. What the fuck was she supposed to do now? Just leave his body in the motel room and get the fuck out? Maybe. She wasn't sure anyone knew she was here in Atlantic City. Had she told anyone? Like who? Who did she have to tell anymore? She'd lost her last job as a housekeeper in Asbury Park weeks before, perpetual tardiness, the story of her life. Don had been there and they'd just… taken off. He'd reassured her everything was going to be okay, that they were in on things together, and even though she'd only met him a few weeks before, she'd believed him. She knew he was a man who got along by his wits, a scammer, a schemer, but who was she to judge? He had been there at the exact right moment and, despite all indications to the contrary, she still believed in providence. Did Don tell anyone where they were going? She didn't even know who he had in his life. Parents, siblings, *kids*? They didn't talk about things like that, didn't talk about much. Lived in the moment.

She lay in the bed beside him, closed her eyes. She would have to wipe away all traces of herself from the room, her fingerprints on everything. She imagined getting up and going to the store for cleaning supplies and felt herself drifting off.

When she woke up, Don was still dead. She peeled the sheet down off his body. He was shirtless but wore his black underwear. They were tight. The rest of his body looked like a sausage, faint red and blue veins and arteries just under the surface of his pale skin. His tufted chest hair. She was tempted to take off his underwear and take a look at his cock one last time. It was one of the most middling cocks of her life. Not big, not small. Soft, it curled up like an anemone. She resisted the urge, for now.

Got up, drank water out of one of the motel room cups, looked at his pile of clothes by the side of the bed. Her head hammered. The vodka bottle, a fifth of Popov, was empty but she upended it anyway, got maybe a drop, felt like crying. She picked up his clothes and went through the pockets, found his old black leather wallet, smooth and rounded at the corners. Surprised to see it jammed full of bills. It was dirty money, not money he'd won and not told her about at the casino. Nearly three hundred dollars. Two-hundred-ninety-seven to be exact. Charl felt like crying. Partly from joy. It was better not to parse her emotions, better to simply let them pass through her, water through a duck. There were too many feelings to isolate any one of them. She took out all the credit cards and other cards from their respective slots in the wallet, a panoply of plastic, knew the credit cards were maxed out because he'd tried every single one of them in the last few days. There was his ID. New Jersey State. Relieved to see that his name was, in fact, Don Thompson, like he'd said. Didn't recognize the address in Ramapo. In the inside compartments of the wallet Charl found two pictures of two different little girls. School pictures with smoky gray backgrounds. One kid wore a pink dress over a white shirt, the other kid looked Goth. Charl turned them over, saw their names and ages written in a scrawl. They both looked like good kids, but the second one looked troubled. She knew how good girls could go bad. She put the pictures back. He'd had a whole life she knew nothing about. Was surprised she didn't care more.

Got dressed in a black hoodie and her jeans that used to fit but now had to be held up by Don's old belt. Looked at herself in the mirror. Her eyes were black holes and her skull was starting to show through the skin. Give it enough time and it would. Slick white bone. She turned away, went out to the corner store, got a carton of cigarettes, a container of orange juice, some jerky, a razor, a toothbrush and toothpaste, went and ordered a huge breakfast from the Seaside Grill on the corner, took the plastic container stuffed full of food back into the room.

Don didn't smell yet. She wondered when bodies started to smell. Knew Don's body was already decomposing, even if she couldn't smell it. She was already breathing in parts of him. Which was fine with her. She would take him all in, reconstituted, carry him with her for the rest of her life. What she had known of him was enough to know that she loved him, in a way. At least until last night, when she'd hated him for the first time. That psycho face. Every man was capable of turning, no matter how harmless they seemed. The smell of vomit was faint, and she opened the window while she ate, cold mist filtering through the screen and dotting the fake wood table, her hands. She ate until she puked, shoveling in home fries and French toast and little sausages like dog dicks, then she ate a little more, then she closed the plastic container for later.

Tenderly, she got a washcloth and cleaned the side of Don's face with it. His skin was sandpaper, stubble catching the terrycloth and pulling. She thought of sharks. Then she folded his clothes neatly, threw away the vodka bottle. When a knock came at the door, a jolt of panic shot through her, but then someone said "housekeeping" in a tired but shy Hispanic-tinged voice. "Not now!" she yelled. She empathized—she'd seen some shit in her five-month stint as a housekeeper. She was relieved when the housekeeper moved on to the next door, the rattle of cart wheels on the metal landing. She opened the door, put the Do Not Disturb hangtag on the knob, closed it again. Felt safe and unsafe. Looked around the room. The art on the wall, a single painting, was… not art. It was like a painting produced by a robot. Lifeless. Lines and colors, geometrical. She wished she could disappear inside it.

She rolled Don's body onto its back, covering him with the covers, then she took a long hot shower and thought about Easter. The way, as a girl, she'd dressed in a fancy dress and stood on the driveway with a stuffed bunny in her hands—a picture she'd seen a hundred times before but didn't remember living. Remembered shards of church memories: Easter bonnets, Easter baskets, sermons, lambent light through stained glass. Jesus had risen, but what did he do after that? Rested, she hoped. She remembered ham and dyed eggs, cakes shaped like lambs, a world so distant from this one it could have been science fiction. She wondered how long the hot water would last. Was willing to find out. Let it fall over her body, which had seen better days. Too thin in some places, too fat in others. Why did Don even want her? He didn't anymore. He didn't want anything anymore. She lathered up with the motel soap, shaved her armpits and legs, was tempted to shave her bush the way Don had asked her to a few times but wouldn't. That was unnatural. Not that she hadn't before. Soaped up her hair and let the suds run over her. Felt almost human. The food had helped her head, and she felt her stomach working away at what remained after she puked. It hurt a little. If she could make food a normal thing again. If she could…

She dried off then realized she had no clean clothes to put on. She put her black hoodie, her jeans, her white undershirt, her red underwear into the bathtub, embarrassed by how they looked and smelled, though who was there to be embarrassed in front of? She was alone. Now that she was clean, the clothes smelled worse. Like all the smells from the last four days had seeped inside them. Smoke, of course, but also blood and piss and shit and other unidentifiable but organic odors. The aromascape of Atlantic City. Gross. People they'd walked past the night before had given them a wide berth, wrinkling their nose. Normals. Now she knew why. The water turned gray and brown and red, and she worked like a washerwoman of old, scrubbing and kneading, and scrubbing and kneading, then wringing it all out and hanging it all up to dry from the shower rod.

Naked, she slipped into bed beside Don's dead body. She didn't want to at first but her body did what was natural and she found herself curling against him, her man. He was not warm but wasn't cold yet, the way they said dead bodies got. She wondered how long before that would happen. There was no warmth to him, but she was warm inside the covers and she imagined she lent him some of her warmth.

She dreamed she brought him back to life with the warmth of her own body and she pulled down his black underwear and she slid down onto his hard cock and fucked him as he gasped with the breath of new life. She woke up a little wet and a lot ashamed, and she refused to touch herself even though she wanted to. Hard to tell how long she'd slept because the day was the same gray, but she felt physically better than she had in a long time. She did nothing for a while but simply felt alive. She missed moments like this, when they'd hang out in bed after fucking and just do nothing. No need to do anything. They'd done that a lot in the first few weeks, less and less often recently. She imagined the feel of his fingertips along the surface of her skin, her hips and sides and arms, raising gooseflesh, as if she were something special. Back when he'd been amazed by the physical reality of her. Maybe that was all a put-on, but it felt real.

She would have to do something and soon, but she didn't want to do anything. It was kind of nice having Don like this. He was quiescent. The word came to her unbidden from some former life when she'd read things. She'd been a weird reader kid in middle school. Hard to believe that had been her. Back before things had rolled out of control, a whole series of bad decisions involving boys and men and drugs and liquor. She felt her stomach grabbing hold like a fist, and she went into the bathroom and took the first semisolid shit in at least a week. She looked in the mirror. If she kept up like this she would be back to her old self in no time. She wanted to go out and get fucked up, she wanted a drink or four, but she didn't need that shit anymore. Of course she did.

The money was enough for probably two nights at a motel somewhere and another meal. Maybe some cheap sweatpants. Her clothes were still damp, but she put them on anyway. They felt like someone else's clothes. They still smelled. Some things can't be held back or covered over. She could buy some new clothes, cheap, from the Salvation Army. Could become someone else. A new name. She would still be Charl even if she could convince people to call her Debbie or something. She was not someone who could change like that.

She pocketed the bills and walked out into the night. The Vietnamese woman at the packaged goods store looked at her with narrowed eyes that seemed to breathe the way mouths breathe, a little relieved when she didn't see Don following her, or maybe noticing that Charl was changed now. She bought a liter of vodka, Tito's, a step up from their normal Popov, and a half liter bottle of tonic water, and she went back dangling a black plastic bag from her hand. It was wet outside but not raining, and the same people she'd seen the last four days were all out on the streets. No one said anything to her.

In the motel room she set up two drinks in the plastic motel cups they used for almost everything. She toasted him and drank down one drink, then sat there crying. Once she got that out of her system, she finished the other drink, wiped down the place for her prints, and went out the door, the black plastic bag dangling, leaving the card key on the table and Don decomposing in the bed.

Cam

I turned on the coffee pot as I passed through the kitchen, and the water was gurgling by the time I opened the door to my basement apartment. When Cam didn't come in right away, I looked up at him. Blood covered his hands and was spattered across his t-shirt. That iron smell hit me—like liver, like the inside of a body. His hoodie had no blood on it. He wasn't shaking yet. He stood still, staring straight ahead.

Cam was the steadiest person I knew. A safety on the high school team, he wrecked people—never hesitated, didn't care how big they were. The harder the hit, the more he loved it. I had never seen his eyes anything like this.

I'd left him five hours earlier with a woman we met at a bar. The three of us had ended the night drinking in a field after The Admiral kicked us out following last call. Cam and the woman had been gravitating toward each other all night, ragging on each other the way two people do when they're moving toward an obvious end. We'd been drinking vodka with Coke chasers, looking at the stars. She laughed at everything. I remembered her legs in tight jeans, the way her chin curved. She had the vibe of someone's mother, but she told us to call her Missy.

"What the fuck happened, man?"

Cam blinked, walked in. The ceilings in my apartment were low, and he was six-foot. He went to the kitchen sink, stared at his hands. The blood had dried, thicker in some places. He didn't move until I turned on the faucet for him, made sure it ran warm, held his hands under it. That's when the shaking started. His ballcap was gone, and his hair clumped together in patches. He looked like a little kid, even though Cam had always looked like an adult, even back then.

The sink wasn't enough. I led him to the bathroom, pink water dripping from his fingers, and ran the shower. I helped him undress. I pulled off the hoodie, told him to lift his arms, peeled the bloody t-shirt over his shoulders. The blood had soaked through. I unbuckled his belt, pulled down his jeans. His dick flopped out, but it wasn't sexual—it felt like caring for a sick kid. He looked at me for a second, then stepped into the shower. I stuffed the bloody clothes into a plastic bag and laid out the biggest clothes I had: jeans, a sweatshirt, boxers, socks.

Later, Cam sat in my truck, staring. My sweatshirt fit tight, the sleeves short on his wrists. I'd made eggs and bacon and toast, but feeding him felt like feeding a zombie. He ate some eggs, drank the coffee. I had a hangover, dull and echoing, like being inside a freshly rung church bell.

He didn't speak, just stared at me. "What happened?" I asked.

He shook his head. "I don't know."

"What do you mean you don't know? Did you kill her?"

"Who?"

"Missy." Her name sounded wrong in my mouth. She had blotchy freckles, a narrow face, freckled hands. She had three kids, was divorced, lived in a trailer park. She drank 7 and 7s and worked at the factory outside town, the one that made film for tinted windows. I'd learned all that the night before. Her whole life, reduced to a few facts.

"Oh." He looked out the window. "No," he said after a while.

We drove. Cam lit a cigarette and rolled down the window. November air poured in. The sun cut through the leaves, black shapes in the white light.

I took us up Ritchie Road's switchbacks and parked in our old spot. New growth brushed the undercarriage. We hadn't been up here in a while. Since I got my place, we didn't need to. Cam grabbed the bag of clothes and walked ahead, following the logging trail. We used to come out here to get away from our parents—his dad, my mom. We had parties here. Dozens of kids drinking, blasting Nirvana and Pearl Jam, going wild—fighting, dancing, hooking up. An old foundation still stood, and higher up, the tent we set up last year still leaned like a man with cracked ribs. The firepit was full of charred wood. We gathered deadfall. The leaves underfoot felt right. We were doing something. Together.

Cam started the fire. I dragged two lawn chairs from the brush, one with a busted leg, the other missing some plastic slats.

When the fire grew, Cam pulled the bloody t-shirt from the bag. It had dried stiff, blood hardened into a shape. I told myself maybe it was animal blood. He tossed the shirt into the fire. It hit heavy, almost smothering the flames. Then the edges caught, curled, sizzled. Cam added wood and kept the fire going. He threw in the underwear, then the jeans. The stains on them looked like handprints. Maybe his.

He sat back, eyes on the fire.

"Go get us a bottle," he said. "I want to get drunk."

I wanted to say something sharp—go get it your fucking self—but instead, I drove into town. I bought a bottle of scotch, a bottle of vodka, a bottle of peppermint schnapps. I stopped at Doug's for two Italian subs, chips, and a couple waters. Cam hadn't moved when I got back. His hair still clung to his scalp, matted. I saw his bald spot for the first time—he hadn't taken off his cap in years. The fire blazed, only buttons and rivets left of the jeans.

We got drunk. He hit the vodka. I sipped the schnapps. The sky wheeled above us, and everything tilted.

"Give me your keys," Cam said. I handed them over, followed him through the woods. Drunk, I tasted peppermint schnapps and Italian sub, my sleeves greasy. Trees lurched into my path.

"Where are we going?"

He didn't answer. He'd drank as much as I had, but he didn't stumble. He walked straight to the truck, had it running before I climbed in. He tore out fast, leaves spinning behind us, the truck fishtailing. Branches scraped the sides.

I shoved a tape into the stereo. Alice in Chains blared—"Rooster." Cam didn't flinch. The music felt perfect. He tore down Hell's Delight Road, hugging curves too fast, tires shrieking. I didn't care if we wrecked. If we smashed into a tree or Mr. Grayson's garage, I wouldn't have minded. I knew it could happen, but I didn't believe it would. I sang along, but stopped when I looked over.

Cam's face was blank.

"Bro, what happened?" I said. "Just tell me."

He shook his head and pulled over to the side of the road. He ran to the ditch and threw up, his hands on his legs. Wearing my clothes, he looked like someone different. I thought of all the things we'd done together—growing up in this little town in Western Maryland. Stupid shit. Hunting. Games.

He dropped me off at my apartment in town, and then he took my truck. He didn't tell me where he was going.

Later I would hear about what he'd done to that poor woman, and it would be hard for me to reconcile. The Cam I knew wasn't capable of it. But I'd seen the blood on his hoodie, the handprints on his pants. I'd felt the moment of us turning away from each other in the woods, the before and after stark now, one here, the other out there.

Bodies in Bags

I found the leg in the dumpster in back of Wilddale Elementary at six a.m. Aside from the leg, it was how I started all my workdays: slamming the dumpster around and waking up all the rich assholes in their mini-mansions through the woods. Fuck 'em all.

I only noticed the leg by chance, because I happened to look in the bed of the dump truck before compacting all the trash and noticed the ripped plastic bag and something fleshy and shining in the darkness. *What the fuck* was my first, and natural, response. There was no question about it: it was a body part.

I called 911 and waited for them to get there. It took more than an hour. While I waited, the kids started showing up at the school on their buses. My own kid, Darvon, went to Wilddale, and I hoped he wouldn't notice his mother out by the blacktop smoking a cig and waiting for the forensics team to come, though he was too young to be embarrassed by my job. I knew the world would do that to him soon enough, make him embarrassed of me and my job, but I had a few good years left. I watched the kids get off the bus and scurry into the elementary school that looked like a lot of other elementary schools, red and yellow and blue cinder block.

Finally the forensics team arrived in a big van. They wore hazmat suits, and a couple of them climbed up into the bed of the dump truck with all that trash and started rooting around, and another of them took pictures, and a third laid out a body bag and they placed the leg, or the part of the leg, down there on top of the body bag. It was a woman's leg, a young woman's leg, you're probably not surprised to hear, because bodies in bags almost always belong to women. That's the kind of fucked up world we live in. A world of mostly women's bodies in bags. The leg looked hacked off at both ends, but I didn't get too close a look at it.

I took a pic of the leg, zooming in, and sent it to my girlfriend Tanya, who texted back "WTF!" She was probably in bed, because she sleeps later than me (her job starts at 10 a.m.) and I stood there smoking another cig (I'm trying to cut back) and watching the forensics team and imagined Tanya in the bed, imagined her expansive and complex body. It's still a new enough thing that everything about her excites me, but I don't think it's going to last, and I want to get everything I can out of the relationship.

If it's possible to think about two things at the same time, I thought about Darvon in the school behind me at the same time. He was with his father this week. I imagined him sitting there the way he does with his hands gathered in front of him on the desk. His soft ways worry me. I know he's going to get picked on if he isn't already. Such a sweet kid. Sweet kids get eaten for breakfast in this world.

Adding in a third thing, I also thought about whoever the leg belonged to. I imagined some coed from down near Boston. A recent college graduate living on her own. Blonde and pretty but not too pretty. Her poor parents.

The world was rotten and men were cruel and life ended too soon for too many people, and there I was between things just waiting to move to the next dumpster—this one outside the old age home across town—so my day wasn't backed up any more than it already was.

The forensics team was thorough, but they didn't inspire confidence at all. They were like grown kids playing in dirt. I knew they would find out who the leg belonged to, thanks to DNA and all that shit, but I wished that we lived in a world where people could disappear forever.

The Body in Lake Montebello

January 20, 1958, 7:34 a.m.

It was the kind of cold that seeped into your bones. Dixon stepped out of the warm interior of his black Hudson onto the tarmac path circling Lake Montebello, the water reservoir in east Baltimore, pulling his black wool overcoat tight around him, pressing his hat down over what remained of his hair. The horizon, between breaks in the rowhomes around him, was pink, fading upward into pale blue, and a frigid wind pressed hard against his face. It was Thursday, much earlier than he would have liked. He'd left his pretty new wife, Anne, sleeping in bed after receiving the call.

The body had been pulled half out of the water by the patrolman, an Irishman a few years younger than Dixon. O'Neil, maybe. O'Malley? O'Something. A woman wearing worn black shoes, hair a snarl of gray and brown curls, had found the body. She stood shivering by the side of the path that ringed the lake, eyes distant—as if she'd seen worse.

He'd arrived before the hearse and crime lab folks, who'd take photographs and, if they could find any, shoe tread impressions. He'd also arrived, thank God, before the reporters. Any second now the vultures would descend: photogs from both the *Sun* and the *Daily* would arrive before the body was hauled away.

By the path beside the lake, Dixon asked the woman a few questions, took notes. The time she found the body: 6:30. How the body looked when she first found it: she thought it was a log at first, resting at the edge of the lake, but something told her it wasn't. She'd walked down to the water, noticed a leg sticking out, realized it was a body, found the patrolman sleeping in his car on Hillen.

When he got down to the body, Dixon scanned the ground for footprints. The ground was frozen and wouldn't hold footprints, and no one had dropped anything nearby. It would take a careless criminal to leave something meaningful behind, and judging by the way the body had been packaged this had not been the act of a careless criminal.

Dixon crouched to get a closer look at the body. Wrapped inside a brown blanket, tied tightly with rope, both inside and outside the blanket. He tried to undo the knots, then cut through the ropes with his pocketknife. Peeled aside layers of blanket and a plastic tarp to reveal the head. The top of a black suit, with narrow lapels, and a white shirt, silk tie pulled askew. It was the aspect of the face that surprised Dixon. It was a white man, or at least had been at one time, yet the face was deformed. The nose was no more than two nostrils, almost slits, and there were growths on the forehead. Not what Dixon had expected. Despite its unusual appearance, the face looked at peace, as if the man were simply resting, not dead and drowned. No signs of struggle. It looked perfectly preserved. Which somehow made it even more disturbing.

"What do you think?" he asked O'Something, hovering behind him.

"Beats the hell out of me," O'Something answered. "That's your job."

Dixon nodded, figuring the chances of solving the crime had increased. This was not a man who could walk unremarked down the street.

He walked the crime scene, looking for clues because that was what he was supposed to do, not because he had any hope of finding anything.

He sat awhile in the Hudson with the woman. He took her name and number and told her she was free to leave, but she stayed in the car a little longer, watching as the crime lab people arrived and took photographs.

As expected, before long the vultures descended and took their photographs, of the body, the lake, the rowhomes across the lake, taking up stances like soldiers, as if they were doing something important in the world. A reporter he was familiar with, an older man with white hair named Tompkins, approached the car, but when he recognized Dixon he backed away. Dixon had a reputation among reporters. He'd cold-cocked one a few years earlier outside City Hall, breaking the guy's nose.

He sat inside the Hudson watching as the body was placed on a stretcher and carried away. The sun was full up now, the sky a sodium blue that made Dixon think of Nagasaki and Hiroshima.

He'd grown up thinking the world was going to blow itself up someday. If it weren't for Anne, he would have wished it had.

The city morgue was in the basement of the precinct building on Wabash. There were two ways to get in, three if you counted the bulkhead doors through which bodies were carried. Dixon preferred the back way, through a squat black door so old it had an iron ring for a handle. The stairwell was narrow and dark, and it grew colder as he descended. In the summer that was a relief from unrelenting humidity, but in the winters it was a reminder of the frozen tundra they lived in for several months a year.

Classical music played in the examination room, so Dixon knew Manuel was at work. Chopin, a piano sonata. Dixon was no classical music aficionado, but Manuel had predictable tastes. Chopin and Bizet, Beethoven and Debussy. The coroner would listen to sonatas when starting an examination, opera while writing up his reports or doing busy work.

Manuel was already working on the body when Dixon walked in, greeted by the nostril-clearing scent of formaldehyde. The body was laid out on a table. Manuel had snipped the rest of the ropes around the blanket, opened it and the tarp underneath, like a florist opening a bundle of flowers. The man inside, fully dressed, looked remarkably unaffected by death. The black suit was too big for him, as if he'd bought it on sale or had once been a much larger man. His hands were big and white and looked like working man's hands, while the rest of him was small.

Manuel nodded at the detective.

"Doesn't look dead, does he?" Dixon said.

"Oh, he's dead all right. Don't let him fool you."

Manuel unknotted the tie, sliding it out from the collar, folding it, placing it on a table to the side. The music gave each of his gestures an air of civility. After unbuttoning the white shirt, exposing a bird-like chest, Manuel tilted the big head upward to show Dixon marks on the neck.

"Ligature. Probably choked to death. Definitely a homicide."

"You think?"

"I do, yes."

Sarcasm was lost on Manuel, or else he was a Zen master of it.

As Dixon sat on the stool watching Manuel work, the two men settled into a comfortable quiet. The music ran on, phrases repeating in slightly different ways until they'd completely changed.

The body on the table revealed itself a little at a time, a narrow torso, dark nipples, a surprisingly slim body, a modest penis curled on its side like an anemone nestled inside dark hair. The feet, small and pale, reminded Dixon of a dancer's.

"Could you tell if he was bigger once? Did he lose a lot of weight?"

"Not likely. There's no excess skin. I'd say he's always been about this size."

"There's some skin under his fingernails," Manuel said a while later, showing Dixon the man's hands, one of the fingernails blackened. "There was some struggle, but not very vigorous struggle."

"It doesn't look like he had much fight in him."

"Small guys will surprise you sometimes."

The doc opened the body and started rooting through the organs, pushing viscera here and there. The smell of an opened body seeped into all corners of the room, a smell so rank it almost crawled on hands and feet. Manuel was absorbed in his work and acted like Dixon wasn't there. Dixon told him to call when the autopsy was finished and walked back out into the cold.

Inside the precinct building across town, Dixon took the narrow, coffin-shaped elevator up, accompanied by some little rat in need of a haircut who slipped in just before the doors shut and couldn't stop shaking. He was probably going to inform on someone so he could get enough scratch to buy a bottle, so he could survive a little longer before winding up shot or stabbed in some back alley, or frozen to death if the drink caught up to him before revenge could. He was a foot shorter than Dixon, his skin sallow. He reeked of sweat and piss and wore a flat cap pressed down over his hair. He kept scratching a gash on his neck, and Dixon thought of the marks on the dead man's neck. A ligature. If he'd been strangled, why didn't his face show any sign of struggle?

When they got off the elevator on the third floor, the rat went right while Dixon went left toward the bullpen, the dumping ground for all the unwanted refuse in the other precinct offices, an open room in a corner of the third floor filled haphazardly with desks and filing cabinets. Old coatracks and random pieces of furniture laid around. Homicide took pride in not caring about their surroundings, pretending they were too busy to care. Mostly they were.

Dixon could look out the window and see the backs of City Hall and the courthouse, buildings that had pretensions to classical virtues. Columns and faces carved into the lintels. There were three other detectives in the bullpen at this time of the morning, presumably working cases. Henderson was sitting with his feet up on his desk shoving a sandwich wrapped in wax paper into his mouth. Tollis was talking, low and excited, into the phone. To his bookie, Dixon assumed. Then there was old Brandt, who sat his fat ass in the corner of the room every day and stared out the window awaiting retirement, dreaming of whatever sexual proclivities thrilled him and the white beaches of Florida. Dixon hoped he never got to that point. Take him into some dark alley and shoot him first.

Dixon's desk was in the far-right corner of the bullpen, a desk he'd been given when he first started in the department and kept, even though he could have swapped it. He liked it; it was out of the way. He could disappear into the background. He wasn't grubbing to move up the ladder like most men his age; he was perfectly content where he was.

He sat at his desk, shuffling papers, waiting for the call from Manuel. Figured Anne would be awake by now. Pictured her wearing black pants, the ones that ended just below the knee, fashionable pants that somehow both hid and accentuated her sexuality, pants that were probably too young for her. A lot of things Anne did were too young for her. She kept up. In her early thirties but still a schoolgirl. There were lost years in her past, years he had no idea what she'd been doing. She didn't talk about her past, and he didn't press.

He figured he could go down to Fells and talk to regulars and bartenders at the seedy bars, see if they'd ever seen the freak down there. They'd remember him. But Dixon didn't get the feeling the freak would go in for bars. He wasn't sure why. Just a feeling.

The harsh jangle of the phone caught Dixon's attention. On the phone, Manuel explained what he'd found. Asphyxiation. There was no water in the freak's lungs. He hadn't drowned but, as expected, had been choked to death before being tied up and dumped in Lake Montebello. He couldn't determine how long the body had been in the lake, precisely, but he'd been dead about a week. There were no other injuries aside from the one on his neck. 5'4", 110 pounds. That sounded so small Dixon pictured a miniature man moving through a miniature world.

"One other thing," Manuel said, reluctant to share whatever he was going to share next.

"What's that?"

"There are some, er, abnormalities in the body."

"Meaning?"

"Meaning… He's not exactly human."

At first Dixon thought Manuel was joking, but that wasn't Manuel's way.

"Yeah? What is he then?"

"I have no idea. It's like someone came up with a pretty good approximation of a human."

"Okay."

"But couldn't quite pull it off. It's tricky, the human body."

"Okay."

After thanking Manuel, Dixon put down the phone and looked out the window. The buildings looked fake in the stark light, like a series of geometrical patterns. He didn't know what the hell Manuel was on about, or what it meant for the case, but a sudden wave of dread washed over him.

He went home to Anne and they made love like the newlyweds they were, rattling the bedframe, embarrassing the neighbors. It made Dixon feel alive, but afterward Anne went to the library to do some studying and he was alone again. He put a record on the record player, Miles Davis, *Birth of the Cool*. The body was not quite human. What the hell was that supposed to mean?

The next morning he picked up the papers and was surprised to see no news about the body found in Lake Montebello. He sat at his desk, wondering how to start an investigation into a deformed man no one had ever seen who presumably was not even human. Maybe he could start with the circus, though they hadn't been in town for months.

He got a call around ten o'clock, an unknown voice asking him to meet at a bar in Fells, and when he got there he saw Tompkins, the reporter he'd seen the day before at Lake Montebello, sitting at a table with a whiskey neat. Dixon ordered the same.

"Dixon," Tompkins said. "So, what did you find out about the body in the lake?"

"Why do you want to know?"

"I've got some information that might be of interest to you."

"The body had been choked."

"That's all?"

Dixon shrugged, looked around, infected by the other man's paranoia. He didn't like it, at all. Tompkins nodded and smiled. He looked like he was about two steps from either a vacation or an asylum.

"I know where he came from."

"Is that right?"

"Yeah, that's right. You care to take a look?"

"I guess a good detective follows every lead."

"Pick me up outside the *Sun*. Sundown is 5:22. Pick me up at 4:30 so we can get out there before then."

Dixon nodded, feeling a little woozy from the day drinking.

He decided to surprise Anne at the library. He saw her through the window, wearing a cashmere sweater and black pants, her hair half in her face. She looked like a movie star. He still couldn't believe his luck. Something horrible must have happened to her in the past for her to be happy with him. When she looked up from her book and saw him outside, her face lit up.

"Hey, doll," he said when she came out and wrapped herself around him.

"Hey."

They went to a bar near campus and ordered a simple lunch and a few drinks. She told him what she was studying. The Kwakiutl potlatch. In a potlatch, the tribe gave gifts to the chief, then burned all those gifts. Some renunciation of worldly goods thing.

They parted ways with a sloppy kiss, and he told her he'd be home late, had to stake out an apartment for an investigation. An innocent lie.

Before he knew it, it was 4:00 and he was driving to the *Sun* building, sitting outside in his Hudson, letting the engine run so he could get some modicum of warmth through the vents.

He drove where Tompkins directed him: out of the city, through the countryside, down a dirt road that ended at an abandoned asylum. While he drove, they were mostly quiet. He noticed Tompkins's hand. At first he didn't know why the hand, with fingers splayed across his thigh, seemed odd, but then he realized there was an extra finger on it. It wasn't the pinky or the pointer, could have been either an extra ring or middle finger, though "middle" finger would be inaccurate on him.

They drove out past the asylum, down more dirt roads. Dixon knew no one was to be trusted, but he wasn't worried about Tompkins. He could handle Tompkins and his six fingers.

"Been following the story long?"

"About a year now. And it's gotten to me."

"Yeah? How's that?"

"It gets weirder the longer I'm on it. It starts with a few sightings, then there are all these bodies showing up."

"More than one?"

"This isn't the first."

Dixon nodded, parked, followed Tompkins into the woods. He wore a fedora and a loose gray suit, which, along with the white hair, made him easy to follow. Almost immediately he lost sight of Tompkins on the trail. He was much faster than a man his age should have been, though he didn't seem to exert himself. Dixon, meanwhile, huffed and puffed. The woods got darker fast, but when they emerged, after climbing uphill about a half hour, they were on the spine of what seemed like a small mountain range, though it was probably just a good-sized hill. Below, Dixon could see the Patapsco River and the railroad tracks. It was a pretty sight. Tompkins settled down on the dirt, making himself comfortable, folding his legs Indian style.

"Might take a while," Tompkins said, pulling a flask from his pocket, displaying it and smiling. Dixon, still looped from his day drinks, smiled back and accepted the flask when it was handed to him. They set to waiting.

The next thing Dixon knew he was coming to on the rocks on top of that hill in the dark, his body sweat-soaked, in the dark. Drunker than he'd ever felt in his life. The sky made a whooshing sound above him, but all he saw were stars.

Tompkins nowhere to be seen. Dixon staggered up, veering toward the edge of the rock, almost toppling over before getting his legs underneath him.

The images passing through his mind could not be called memories. They were disjointed, vivid yet somehow unclear. Tompkins laughing, something in the sky, a flash of silver, something smooth and round, something else sharp and jutting. He remembered smells, but they were not smells he'd ever smelled before. Not only unfamiliar but unimaginable. Leaning against a tree trying to get his bearings, he realized his gun was gone. The whooshing was coming not from the sky but from inside his skull.

The trail was steep, areas of scree hard to negotiate in the moonlight. He kept having to scramble. He tried to remember the story Tompkins had been telling before he lost consciousness, about little men infiltrating the human race, how they were trying to take over. He thought of Tompkins's six fingers and his supernormal speed on the trails. The body he'd seen pulled out of Lake Montebello. If not for the body, he would have thought it was all the hackneyed dream of a fevered mind preoccupied with popular culture. There were all kinds of movies about flying saucers, and he'd heard reports. People were dumb enough to believe anything. He wouldn't have believed it if Manuel hadn't told him that the body wasn't human. If there hadn't been a coverup by the newspapermen. He wondered if they were safe, any of them. Before this he'd thought the city was going to pot, but now he wondered if it weren't bigger than that.

He was halfway down the trail when the whooshing in his head separated and came from the sky again. He looked up. Saw a flash. Something swift and stealthy, a shadow more than anything, but a shadow with cognizance, a shadow very clearly *pursuing* him. He tried to run, his feet uncertain on the scree, ankles wobbling. He kept to the shade of trees, but that made it impossible to see anything. Whatever the shadow was, it was onto him, getting closer, the sound moving through the air and getting into his head.

Hours later, he slid into bed. He felt his body shaking, then taking in the warmth of the blanket, the warmth of Anne's body, slowly calming.

When she turned to smile at him, he saw too many teeth in her mouth. She was like a shark with rows and rows of teeth.

Dream a Little Dream

Dream a little dream of me. Tom Atkinson drives through blown-out pinelands at dusk, whispering the words then singing at a normal volume. Dream a little dream of me. It's a stupid song, but it tugs at something deep inside him. A girl sang the song to him a few months after he returned from 'Nam. Back then he thought he was in love. Talk about stupid.

The woods flanking the road are thick but young, pines and cedars competing for space. C*ome on and love me, baby.* That girl had been out of her mind, crazy as a loon, bat-shit crazy. Crazy, anyway. One day after returning from work, Tom found her in the bathtub, blood spooling out from her slit wrists, pink spreading slow through tepid water. He'd carried her to his truck wrapped in his flannel robe, weighing hardly anything, dripping, driven her to the hospital. He wonders where she is now.

Dream a little dream of me. The wheel wells of his Ford F-150 coated with dried mud as he drives, both windows half-open, south Jersey air filling the cab. He pops the dashboard lighter in, lights the end of a Camel. Sections of the pinelands smell like sap while other sections, especially as he nears the shore, possess the rotten-egg stench of sulfur. Smell of his youth. The sound of the piano is barely there. Nothing showy about it. He appreciates it.

The song ends, replaced by an equally insipid song, and he switches off the radio. The rush of wind takes the place of silence. The cooler in the bed of the pickup is filled with venison from a deer shot two nights earlier. A rafter of wild turkeys huddle by the side of the road, waiting for the truck to pass, and a small weather-beaten American flag flaps in the middle of a small pond. A cranberry bog blood-red in last light.

The girl had been small and often smelled rank, the funk getting in Tom's nose as they fucked. *What did you see over there?* Her number one topic of conversation. Not *Did you kill anyone?* but *What did you see?* What he'd seen: a fractured people. Enemy and allies identical. Anger hidden behind impassive faces. You couldn't trust anyone, not even kids. Especially kids. You couldn't trust your heart so you had to stomp on it, stop it from influencing your actions. It was all about the mission, protecting your fellow soldiers, your brothers in arms. He didn't see any of them anymore. Stevenson, Harper, Longo. She'd clawed his chest and bit his neck while he carried her around the room, her ass in his hands. She was not a hippie but did serious drugs, tried to get him to do them, too, but alcohol was enough for Tom. Whiskey and beer. He'd had a job then, separating letters in the post office like a feeb, knowing it wasn't going to last, hours passing like prison time.

He flicks his cigarette out the window, red embers splashing a warning sign on the macadam behind him: there, then gone. Jeannie opens the door, tight jeans molded to her strong lower body, work boots, a loose orange sweater, face scrunched, as if he smells like shit. He probably smells like cold field, blood, and gunpowder.

"What the hell are *you* doing here, Tom?"

She takes the poorly butchered venison, wrapped in bloody butcher paper, he proffers. She looks insulted, like the time he showed up with bags of groceries a few months after his brother passed. She's the kind of woman has to do things on her own.

"Good to see you too, Jeannie. What a greeting. Can't a guy pay a visit to his brother's family?" He makes his smile harmless, but it doesn't sit right on his face, his face not a face where smiles sit. Jeannie turns away to grab him a beer from the fridge before lighting a cigarette. She looks better than when Frank was alive, has done a reconstruction job on herself. Hair shoulder length, blonde highlights, ass snug inside jeans. She's been working out. She can't do anything about her face, bearing the tell-tale marks of middle-age, lines etched around eyes and mouth, neck going slack, two tendons around her throat more prominent, but her body looks younger, fresher, firmer, highly fuckable. She knows what she has and is going to use it while it lasts.

"There's this thing called a phone. You should try using one sometime. Give me some warning."

"What do you need warning for?" He smiles. He knows she can see the devil inside him. "Come on, now, you're not really mad at me for showing up out of the blue. We're family. Besides, I couldn't remember your number."

He drinks half the can of beer in one go. He feels like an avenging god, almost. There were times during a firefight when he felt like that. Everything became sharper, more real, when people were shooting at him. That weird manipulation of time, both faster and slower than usual, reality become changeable.

"Hunting season starts *next* week." Jeannie nods down at the venison, a bone-in saddle steak. There's no way she's going to let it go to waste, poached or not, but she has to let him know she doesn't approve.

He shrugs, tries to smile again, Tom Atkinson's weak charm offensive.

She gets a black skillet out from a cabinet, ill-stacked pots and pans clattering, takes down a clear green bottle of olive oil, ass stretching her jeans as she reaches up.

His brother built himself a solid house, an enviable piece of work. He'd built his life around himself, then died. Ironic, almost. The wide-plank pine floors need refinishing, but they're well put together, not half-assed the way so many houses are today. The lighting fixture, with its curved arms and glass covers shaped like flowers, is too fancy for the kitchen, probably Jeannie's choice, but Tom feels comfortable here. Like this is a place he could have built himself, a life he could've had. He sits looking at his hands around the beer can while Jeannie chops at a cutting board, the knife making clean, close cuts. She works at a restaurant, and it shows.

"You going to tell me what's really going on, Tom?"

"Nothing. Nothing is going on."

She shakes her head but doesn't push it. Soon the smells of onions and garlic mix in the room, thick green scents infiltrating everywhere. Jeannie is turned away from him, ass at eye level. He admires it. Hate can lead to good, rough fucking. It's happened before—with other women who hated him.

He gets up, paces the downstairs of the house, feeling caged, something bunched inside him refusing to unfurl. The living room is dark, an old TV the focal point, an easy chair, a loveseat, not much else. He leans in the doorway between kitchen and living room.

"Where's Hunter got himself to?"

"Probably out with his friend Bobby. But he'll be home for dinner. The boy likes his food."

Tom lights another cigarette, moves the ashtray to the counter, leans there. The events of two nights before come back to him: the ranger's truck, the spotlight. He hears the voice shouting at him again, feels himself running back to his pickup, lifting the rifle to his shoulder. Sighting in on the ranger's face. The ranger looked like a kid in the lit-up field. So much white light the black sky was swallowed inside it. Everything frozen white. *Don't move or I'll shoot.* A voice trying to convince itself it was tough and disciplined, repeating words heard in some movie. Tom could feel the truth. That pinpoint accuracy of sight and sound. The rattle of shots fired. His, the ranger's. Blood sluicing through veins. Adrenaline. The tension of it all, the perfect clarity. Everything for that one moment right there in front of him. One of the bullets found the ranger's forehead, a hole appearing in the front and a larger hole busting through the back of his skull big enough to fit a fist through. The body going down hard and heavy with the finality that spoke of death. The ranger was young, probably had kids, definitely had a wife, wedding ring glinting on his finger.

By the time the venison is ready, the kid's home. His brother's kid, there can be no doubt about it. Hunter has Frank's low-set brows and his startling blue eyes beneath them, some combination of bullheaded and vulnerable that had always worked well with women and sometimes got him in trouble with men, who thought he wasn't as tough as he was. Frank liked to fight, or claimed he did. Though it was Tom who went to 'Nam.

Hunter is sullen, sitting with fork and knife grasped in each hand, looking over at his uncle now and then, hair too long in front, getting in his eyes.

"What do you say, Hunter?"

Hunter shrugs, looks confused, a little scared, shoots a glance at his mother then back at Tom.

"Not much, Uncle Tom."

"That's the truth," Jeannie says.

She puts some music on the stereo in the other room, and they eat listening to Waylon Jennings, probably from Frank's CD collection.

Out back in the shed, Tom is impressed with his brother's tool collection and the way he kept it. There's a station for woodworking. Hasps, a jigsaw, a lathe, a sander, a bandsaw, a miter saw. There are cigar boxes filled with nuts, bolts, screws of all kinds and sizes, each kind and size getting its own box. In one corner is a snowblower and a lawnmower and the various things one needs to maintain them, spark plugs, oil filters. Overhead lights strung up on exposed beams, an old comfortable couch, a minifridge. It's the opposite of Tom's shed back in PA, a simple dark space with barely room enough to hang a deer's body. Frank must have spent hours out here.

In the far corner is a gun cabinet he built with ornate scrollwork on the doors. A scene of reeds, geese flying in a V above them. The cabinet is locked, but Tom finds the keys on a ring in the top drawer of the work desk. Opens the cabinet. Five hunting rifles. A Remington 870, a Browning A5, a Winchester SX4. Two other shotguns. He takes the Mossberg break-action from its stand. It's an old gun they once shot with their father, when he was still alive. Each of the guns appears pristine, though no one has touched them for a year. Before that, Frank had handled them like prized possessions.

He's aware of the kid's presence at the shed door behind him, can feel the cool air streaming in.

"What are you doing?" The kid's voice quiet but clear.

"This gun was both of ours. I'm not taking anything that's not mine."

He hears the hesitation in the boy, a decision being made, feels sorry to have put him in this position, but not really sorry.

"Okay."

"I'm not asking permission."

The boy wears a hooded black sweatshirt with some kind of writing Tom can't decipher—a band name, he assumes—and dirty jeans. He peers out from under his fringe of hair.

"You ever go hunting anymore?" Tom asks.

"No. Not since."

"Would you go with me if I took you?"

Again that hesitation.

"Yeah."

"Maybe we'll do that then."

He carries the Mossberg to the worktable, where there are gun cleaning supplies, neatly arranged. An oil cloth, bore rods, spear-pointed jags, cleaning solvent. The gun is almost pristine, but he breaks it apart and cleans it anyway, ramming the cloth through the two bores, holding the barrel up to look through it. Then he goes to the bandsaw, makes sure the blade is the one he needs, its teeth jagged for metalwork, starts it up. Aware all the time of Hunter standing behind him watching, a dark presence like an occlusion of the eye. He uses the bandsaw to cut down the barrel of the Mossberg, feels a little guilty doing so. He's losing a part of his past here. He's willing to let it all go. The cut is rough but easy. He turns off the whining bandsaw, starts up the belt sander. Wonders how long this equipment will last if no one uses it, why Jeannie hasn't sold it yet. It's all high-quality equipment, worth a few thousand dollars. The belt sander smooths the rough end of the cut-off barrel.

In the gun cabinet, he opens a large drawer, finds shotgun shells, takes three boxes out, stacks them on the workbench.

"Why don't you go get me a beer? And get one for yourself."

The boy says nothing but leaves, slow and lumbering, like a spirit from the underworld. What is it with kids, Tom wonders. He never even came close to having one himself. It's not too late, but it may well be.

They sit for a while drinking their beers when the boy returns, Hunter on the old couch, Tom on a stool by the worktable, silent, the presence now of his brother, of Hunter's father, hovering between them. Frank was a good, simple man. Hunter has no idea what to say to him, and Tom likewise. Tom takes out and lights a cigarette.

"You smoke yet?"

Hunter shakes his head. Their eyes meet. There are things inside there Tom can't begin to fathom, some darkness moving around. Maybe some light, too. They are kin, but there's nothing akin in their minds. He recognizes the character, if not the costume, of loss. He wonders if the boy is slow or crazy, or if this is just the way kids his age are.

"Your father was a good man." Smoke purls out of his mouth into the clean space.

"I know. You're not staying, are you?"

"The night? I'm staying the night."

"After that?"

"I'll be out of your hair soon enough, boy. And your mother's."

Hunter looks at him. Nods slow. He leaves the beer half-drank on the floor, walks out.

Tom carries the sawed-off shotgun and three boxes of shells to the truck, opens the passenger side door, wedges the gun under the seat, wedges three boxes in with it. Shoves a flannel shirt that was on the floor of the cab against the gun. It won't stop anyone from finding the shotgun if they search his truck, but they won't casually see it if they just happen to pull him over. If they know who he is, what he's done, it won't make much difference. He'll be able to get to it if he needs to. He hopes it will give him some comfort as he drives.

There's what looks to be a game trail in back of the outbuilding, and Tom walks it in the near dark of a moonlit night. The land, thick and loud, is familiar. Not hunting season so he doesn't have to worry. He spent as much of his childhood as he could in woods like this. Hunting with his father and Frank, once he was old enough. It was hard hunting, but that made it more worthwhile when you bagged something. Anything worth doing is hard, his father told him.

He walks maybe a mile in the woods, but there's nothing to see except the penny flash of wild eyes, there then gone. He is not quiet. The forest is flat and infinite. If he had to guess, this is what the afterlife his brother went to looks like. Endless walking through endless woods. He doesn't know if this would be purgatory or Hell, but he knows it isn't Heaven.

The man sits at the kitchen table where Tom sat earlier in the evening, like a taller, thinner ghost of Tom's earlier self. Flannel shirt, sleeves rolled over forearms, blue tattoos indecipherable in the dim glow of the hanging light. Cigarette smoke hangs heavy in the room, and Jeannie and the man lean toward each other like two people who have some claim on each other. The man, his lantern jaw dusted with stubble, looks up when Tom walks in. An instinctive repulsion moves through him.

"Who're you?" The words automatic.

"This is Sheeler," Jeannie says.

"Sheeler?"

"Robert Sheeler."

"Bobby Sheeler?"

"At one time," the man shrugs, a smile failing to rise to the occasion.

"Bobby Sheeler," Tom says again, the name familiar even if the man himself is not.

Sheeler runs the edge of his cigarette around the rim of the brass ashtray on the table. The sound of Hunter's music comes sudden, loud, and muted from upstairs. Something even harder-edged than what they'd once listened to. Frank's outlaw county, Tom's hard rock. Tom gets a beer and sits down, uninvited.

"What's the topic of conversation?"

Sheeler narrows his eyes, inhales the last of his cigarette before snubbing it out.

"I'll see you tomorrow, Jeannie?"

"I'll see you tomorrow, Sheeler."

More play in their voices than he'd like. Familiarity, at least. He feels something creep up the back of his neck. It's all too easy to picture the two of them together, in a variety of capacities. The man barely avoids bumping Tom's shoulder when he stands.

"Call me if you need anything," he says to Jeannie.

"I'll be fine."

They sit for a while without saying anything.

"He always listen to that shit?" Gesturing toward the ceiling.

"Most of the night." She shrugs. "It's a way of coping, I guess."

"We all have our ways."

"I'm going to watch some TV, then I'm going to bed, Tom. I'm tired. I worked all morning, and I have to work again tomorrow."

"It's a tough life."

"It really is."

Fifteen minutes later she's in the living room wearing sweatpants and a sweatshirt, letting the TV suck out her soul. He can tell she has one. She watches a show about cops in California chasing some perverted serial killer. It's shot all stylish and flashy, noir, he guesses. He sits down and watches with her but has no idea what's happening and doesn't bother trying to figure it out. He watches her out of the corner of his eye, imagining things.

There's a report on the 11 o'clock news about the funeral being held for the ranger shot and killed outside Gettysburg. They talk about the "thin green line" of officers all coming together to pay their respects for their fallen compatriot. They're a joke, Tom thinks. Jeannie watches without reacting. The reporter says they're still searching for suspects in the murder of the ranger, shot in the line of duty.

Tom was a grunt in 'Nam, traveling mostly through the south of that country with his platoon. He'd seen some shit he will never get out of his head. It comes back to him at idle moments. It always will. Sometimes he gives it room to live again, but mostly he lets it run in the background, like someone else's memories.

Halfway through the news, Hunter's music switches off. Tom had forgotten it was on.

"Good night, Tom," Jeannie says. She heads down the hallway toward the bedroom she and Frank shared.

"You need some company in there?"

She turns to look at him. She looks older than when she opened the door for him. The disgust doesn't help.

"You can't blame a man for trying, can you?"

"You're leaving tomorrow?"

"I'm leaving tomorrow."

"There's bedding in the closet."

"Sure. Good night, Jeannie."

"Good night, Tom."

After she closes the door, he hears her working the lock. He pictures her slipping out of her sweatpants, into the bed. There's something like an ache in his chest, but it goes away. He half-watches a late movie, something black and white and Italian. He doesn't pay attention to the plot but watches the women, otherworldly beautiful.

After the movie ends, he slides back outside. He uses a flashlight Frank kept in the kitchen so he doesn't have to turn the lights on again and wake anyone. He takes out the Winchester and a box of 12-gauge shells, carries them to his truck, backs out quickly so the sound of the motor doesn't bother his sleeping kin too long. Drives two miles, down near the Tuckahoe River, finds the entrance of the dirt road only locals know about, and not all the locals. Drives slow over rutted dirt packed from other truck tires, the foliage on either side overgrown, brushing the side of the F-150; no one has been out here in years. He parks, turns off the headlights. Windows rolled down. It's cool but not cold. The sulfur smell has almost become habitual for him again. He barely smells it. Won't smell it at all by morning.

The girl had blamed him for saving her life. The first look she gave him in the hospital after they put her in a room and stuck an IV in her, he knew it was over, that she hated him now, with a hatred that would never turn to love again. What was he supposed to do? Let her bleed out in his bathtub? He thought of her body in the water. A series of pinks. He hadn't felt anything at all when he looked at her. Maybe irritation, that he was being forced to act. Now he realizes that was shock, allowing him to act at all. Bandaging her wrists. Wrapping her in his flannel robe. He remembers times before that when they'd sat around his apartment, both fucked up in their separate ways. Hard to believe he thought that was love, but he had. He'd pictured them together in a way that could never make sense. She would never be the person he imagined.

He might have dozed off a little in the cab of the truck, but for most of the time he sits looking at the reeds in front of the river, waiting. Finally the light shifts. He feels it more than sees it: dawn. The iterative turnings of the earth. Never-ending and exhausting. He gets out of the truck, stretches. Can stay out here only so long without coffee. There are geese migrating in great numbers, but he doesn't have the will to get the Winchester out.

He gets coffee and a breakfast sandwich from Hark's, in what was once a train depot but is now the dead center of the small town. A throwback kind of place. It could be the 40s or 50s, the shelves half-full of needful things. Bread and cereal. A small cooler with milk and orange juice. Fresh-laid eggs. Behind the counter Hark himself, old now, at first not recognizing Tom, then not making a big deal out of recognizing him. Men who work road crews, construction, and landscaping order breakfast sandwiches, eyes bleary, some laughing together.

Tom sits in the parking lot eating the sandwich and drinking the coffee then lights a cigarette and sits some more, watching people go in and out of the place. He thinks of Hark's life, the last fifty years of it spent in the same town, in the same store. Standing in place while the world spins around him. What kind of life was that?

As he throws the wax paper from the breakfast sandwich and the coffee cup into the garbage can in front of Hark's, he notices the red Mazda pulling into a spot beside his truck. Jeannie in the same clothes she wore the night before, not a work uniform.

"Morning, Jeannie."

"Morning."

"I thought you were working in the morning."

"Afternoon shift, if it's any of your business."

He makes a face that says it's not, just a question. "I'll see you around."

She nods, rushes past him. He sits in his truck, listening to the oldies station. *I found my thrills. On Blueberry Hill.* He lets it play slow and quiet. It's a quiet simple piano he likes now, where he used to like heavy distorted guitar. It's the way of life: change. Nostalgia. He sees Jeannie at the counter laughing with Hark. She must light up the place. Then he watches her open the door with her backside and edge out, carrying two coffees, something in a white bag clutched in her fist. When she sees him sitting there, something happens to her face she tries hard to hide.

"Tell Hunter I'll be by soon to take him hunting," he says through the open window. She nods, arranges her things, backs out of the parking lot, the red Mazda an anomaly in the little town. Like something that wants to be somewhere else. He thinks about following her but decides against it.

The house is unlocked, just as he'd suspected it would be. It feels different empty. He climbs the wooden stairs to Hunter's room. There are posters on the walls, a zebra skin rug on the floor. Some of the posters are of men dressed like women standing in front of what look like Satanic symbols. Mötley Crüe, Megadeth. Other posters are of women, centerfolds, probably from his father's stash of magazines. Women out of the decade before shot in soft focus, their beavers full and resplendent. A few books and magazines scattered here and there. *Creem* and one or two *Soldier of Fortune*. A stereo system with CDs piled everywhere. The room smells of feral boy.

Downstairs, in what was once Frank and Jeannie's but is now only Jeannie's bedroom, he can no longer feel the presence of his dead brother. Two bedside tables, one clear, one with a couple books Jeannie must be reading, an alarm clock. The bedroom is toward the back of the house, and with the blinds open it feels like it's in the woods. He lies on the bed; she will be able to tell he was there. He turns on his side, imagines waking up next to her. He goes through her drawers, reaching under her underthings, half cotton and utilitarian, half lacy or printed, apparently brand new. He finds a Kimber Pro Carry II and a butterfly knife. In another drawer he finds a journal he leafs through. He can't read her handwriting. It might be shorthand.

There's a small, squat safe in her closet, brushed by a few dresses he doubts she ever wears. He could carry it away if he wanted to but doesn't. He memorizes the simple layout of the house. Takes an apple off the counter and bites into it as he walks out.

It's still early, maybe ten o'clock, but he can't wait any longer, so he drives down 55 until coming to the house set far back from the road, an old house that once stood on the carriage road between Atlantic City and Cape May, a historic structure. Looking at it, one can tell it was moved, a long process involving jacks and flatbed trailers. It's settled a little sideways. Dark and foreboding, it sits on the lot next to a restaurant in a low building, the Calvert Cafe, a place that has seen many iterations but is now a fine dining establishment featuring venison steaks and Caesar salads, attached to a dark working class bar where locals drink.

A half dozen cars are parked outside the house, half in working condition, though he can't tell which half. Two trucks not dissimilar to his F-150, a couple low Fords, a Chevy. The pinelands that back up to the house identical to the ones behind Frank's house. Maybe he should feel more urgency in getting himself out of sight, but Tom feels secure in the knowledge that they won't be on his trail yet. Soon, but not yet.

A small, squirrelly man appears at the door before he even gets out of his truck. At first Tom thinks he doesn't know the man, but then he recognizes it's Tim Greeley, a fellow Vietnam vet, though that was about the only thing they shared. Greeley had always been kind of fucked up, but the war tipped him even further in that direction, pushed him down into it. He wears a black t-shirt and blue jeans, and Tom is sure he has a gun on him. He holds the door open only as far as it takes his head to peak out.

"Tom Atkinson."

"Tim Greeley."

"Surprised you recognize me."

"I'm good with faces. Sometimes names."

"What do you want?"

"I want to talk to Sampson. What do you think I want?"

"About what?"

"I'd like to keep that between me and him."

Tim looks at Tom's face, his rumpled clothes.

"Let me talk to him."

After a few minutes, Greeley returns and leads him down into the basement, even darker than the rest of the house. The place reeks of pot and spilled beer. It brings back sense memories Tom would rather not remember. He's spent many nights in this basement, before and after 'Nam. It's been years, yet here he is again. His life keeps circling. Or spiraling, because things change, too, like his brother dying. He doesn't know whether the spiral is going up or down. Down, he suspects.

The basement is the same as it ever was. Pool table, television set, couches, a small kitchen in back. The first thing he notices is the woman—he hopes it's a woman, not a girl—passed out on the couch, under a blanket, head turned toward the back of the sofa, blondish hair a ball with a dent in it. Sampson is stretched out beside her, wearing sweatpants and a black tank top, greasy black hair a fringe in front of his face. His arms are bigger than ever, the biceps like stuffed sausages, with tats running over them in reds, blues, and purples. His legs are thin. Like he only ever does curls. He looks like he just woke up, which is almost definitely the case.

"Atkinson."

"Sampson."

"I was sorry to hear about your brother."

"Yeah. Can we talk?"

"Of course we can talk. We go back a long way."

"Privately?"

"Sure. See you, Greeley."

Greeley looks back and forth from one man to the next as he backs away toward the stairs.

"Don't worry about her. She's out cold."

He proceeds to tell Sampson what he needs: a place to stay, some protection if the Pennsylvania State Police start nosing around.

"I still got that place out in the marsh. You can stay there. But I need something in return."

"What's that?"

"I'll let you know. I think I have a job for you."

"Sure," Tom says, even though he knows all too well what a job for Sampson entails. The last job paid for his trailer up near Gettysburg. He'd tried to get away, but apparently Gettysburg wasn't far enough.

The place is down a long dirt road, following a single strand of electric wire strung from pole to pole. Past pinelands and into deep marsh. No one has been out here in months, maybe years. A hunting cabin in the wetlands. The day has risen hot for fall; gnats swarm everywhere. The smell he was supposed to get used to is still here, worse than ever. Sulfur. Maybe it's a bad day for it.

He carries the Winchester and a box of shotgun shells into the cabin with him. Opens all the windows. The screens are holey, but he has to air the place out. It's musty, smells like something has died in the back room. There are only two rooms, a bedroom backed up to the marsh, everything else in one large square room in front. This house was also built by one person, but not as well as Frank's. Built by someone drunk, lazy, or incompetent, likely all three. A good-enough carpenter whose seams are coming undone. An old wood-framed couch that folds down into a bed. A small, wooden table with one leg shorter than the others. He carries in the groceries he got at the Acme in Somer's Point, enough food to last a month if he's parsimonious and doesn't mind losing a few pounds. A box of whiskey bottles he bought at the Somer's Point liquor store, where the man behind the counter didn't recognize him. The only one who'd recognized him was Hark, and he knows Hark will keep his mouth shut.

Solitude has never been a problem for Atkinson. He learned to master it following the war. He can sit doing nothing for hours, and in the marsh there's a lot of nothing to do. An old plastic-slatted lawn chair that folds up is set up in back of the hunting cabin. The river seems quiet at first but is in fact loud with a million different crepitations. On his second day, Tom finds a duck blind and shoots a duck out of the sky with the Winchester, wades out into the marshes to get it, plucks and prepares it, cooks it over the fire, eats it while the sun goes down behind him, the sky purpling in front of him, one of the best meals of his life, greasy, fatty, real. He wonders if he's hiding out for nothing, if he was wrong and they aren't on his trail, if he'd been imagining things that day he left his trailer. He doesn't think so.

Two weeks into his hermitage, Sampson and his goons show up. Sampson wears sweatpants and a black tank top, like the last time Tom saw him, some kind of uniform for him, and he brings in three other men, one of them Greeley, and two women who are already drunk. They take over the cabin and set to drinking in earnest, playing music on a little boombox. Tom drinks along with them but keeps his distance, doesn't say a word all night.

In the morning, Sampson pulls Tom aside. They walk out by the marsh.

"You know Bobby Sheeler?" Sampson asks.

"Sure I know Bobby Sheeler."

"I want you to take care of him."

Tom nods in understanding, not necessarily agreement.

"Has anyone been around?"

"Yeah, people have been around. Asking about you. You killed that ranger up in Gettysburg."

"Is that what they're saying?"

Sampson gives him a look: don't bullshit me.

"Why Bobby Sheeler?" Tom asks.

"Why do you need to know?"

"I guess I don't."

"I guess not. You take care of Sheeler for me, I can get you set up with what you need to get the hell out, start a new life. New ID, Social Security, passport, let's say five grand. Maybe you can head down to Mexico."

After they leave, Tom thinks through his options. He can't stay in the marsh forever. He could winter here easy, but how long does he want to live in a cabin by himself? He could flee now, but eventually they'd catch up with him. Unless he changes his identity, he will leave a trail behind him they can easily follow, no matter how careful he is. One option: put the barrel of the Winchester to his skull and blow his brains out. No one would care. But something stops him from doing that. Some ghost inside the mechanism. Something inside him, despite everything it knows about life, still wants to live.

He wakes at night and senses a strangeness in the air around him, something he hasn't felt since coming to the cabin, and when he walks outside he's surprised to see shifting lights in the sky, white and slow-moving like living things. They're there, then they're gone, and it's like he's glimpsed something from the other side.

He's sitting in Jeannie's kitchen when she comes out of the bedroom in the morning. He hears Hunter upstairs rustling around, the thud of a living body, like a sloth falling from a tree. The dawn is pink and red, but there's no way to tell that from inside the house. It could be five o'clock still. When she turns the corner, he senses her trying not to react to his presence, to play it cool, but a frisson of fear passes through her. She raises her hand to push a hank of blondish hair out of her face and pulls the robe tight around her. She wears sweatpants and slippers, but he's sure she's bare-chested under the robe; he tries not to let that affect him.

"I woulda made coffee, but I didn't want to wake you."

"That was kind of you. What the hell are you doing here, Tom?"

"Can't you just be nice to me once in your life? Maybe I'm doing you a favor here."

"What kind of favor could you do for me?"

"Make us some coffee and I'll tell you."

She ties the robe around herself, tight, and goes about making the coffee. It's a Mr. Coffee, so easy. Then she slides down a box of cereal, pours some for herself. Holds the box up as an offering.

"I'm good."

The boy, Hunter, slinks into the kitchen, cutting eyes at Tom and his mother, looking like something pried off the ocean floor. Is this what kids are like in the morning? It would drive Tom out of his mind.

"What are *you* doing here?"

"You too? I'm just checking in with my family. My sister-in-law, my nephew. You're all the family I have left."

Jeannie puts a bowl of cereal in front of her son's face.

"Anybody come around looking for me?"

"Yeah."

"What did you tell them?"

"That we hadn't seen you since my dad died."

"That's not exactly true."

"Of course not," Jeannie says. "You wanted us to tell them the truth?"

"No. Thank you." He can sense their discomfort with his sincerity: they both look over at him.

"Where have you been?"

"Nevermind that. I got something to tell your mother."

Hunter finishes shoveling cereal into his face, grabs his backpack, hunkers down inside his black hoodie, disappears. Tom has a bad feeling about him, but he isn't going to say that to Jeannie. She goes back and changes into her waitress uniform then comes out, stands at the doorway waiting.

"Come sit down."

"I'm in a hurry, Tom. Work. You remember that?"

"You don't want to sit down?"

"I don't want to sit down."

He nods. "How close are you and Bobby Sheeler?"

"I don't think that's any of your business."

"It's not, but I'd like to know anyway. Is he…"

"Is he fucking me? Yes, Tom, he's fucking me."

"That's not what I was going to ask."

"He's changed a lot. He's a good man now."

"I believe you. I guess that's all I needed to know. Do you see a future with him?"

She sighs. Closes her eyes. "It's hard for me to see any future at all, Tom. It might seem like I'm jumping into another relationship right after Frank died, but this last year has felt like ten. It's been hard. I don't know if this thing is serious, but I know it's good and that I need it."

Tom nods, looks at his hands around the empty coffee mug.

"Lock up when you leave."

"I will. See ya, Jeannie."

"See ya, Tom."

He sits for a while longer, flashing back to the kid he shot in the field near Gettysburg. The glint of gold from his wedding ring. He can't begin to imagine what kind of woman would marry him. Maybe someone who looked young for her age, a simple woman. Maybe a student at one of the state colleges. What does he know? He imagines a new life: married, a job. He thinks about a kid he shot in 'Nam. Probably thirteen years old, skinny and scared. He shot him in the face and watched his skull shatter. He has been the instrument of death before. He shot a man for Sampson after coming back from 'Nam and hadn't felt much of anything.

The Governor's Inn is a tavern on the water that has stood there since the eighteenth century, a crusty place where working men go to drink after their shifts and tourists flock in summer. Tom sits at the bar ordering another double from the Australian bartender. He can tell the accent works well for him: men don't mind it and women fall all over it. He gets all the pussy he can handle and more. They talk music a while. The Aussie plays guitar in a Led Zeppelin cover band. He's been tending the same bar since before Tom moved to Gettysburg.

He watches the men at the bar. There are two with dark hair and thick forearms. Three linemen. One older woman with thick black hair piled on top of her head and a lined face who keeps looking at him. Maybe someone he knew a lifetime ago.

Bobby Sheeler comes in with two other men in flannel shirts, and they order oysters and a bucket of beer. Sheeler is thin, addiction still apparent around his eyes. He hasn't changed at all, as far as Tom can see. When he spots Atkinson across the bar, his first reaction is to squint, but then he smiles and nods. Tom nods back, one curt dip of the head. It feels strange to be around people after so long alone. He feels like he's not quite there, like he's in some kind of dream state. He felt that way off and on in 'Nam, and ever since. Like a part of him might have died somewhere in the past and the rest of him is just hanging on, living some kind of illusory life.

After an hour or so, the oysters gone, all but one beer in the bucket gone, Tom steps outside to his truck. He moves it to a spot where he can see the entrance of the Inn and waits.

He's not good at imagining, but he imagines himself in Mexico after this is all over, bearing another name. Cobbling together some kind of life. Some life is better than no life, he supposes. He imagines meeting a girl with dark hair, simple, maybe very simple. They could lie around in bed. He could figure out a way to make money somehow. He thinks of the girl he carried out to his truck after she tried to kill herself in his bathtub. Love? Maybe. What did it matter?

When Bobby Sheeler comes out of the Governor's Inn, Tom watches him walk across the parking lot, get into a Silverado, drive off, and he follows, not caring if Sheeler knows he's being tailed. The Winchester leans against the seat beside him, loaded, the Mossberg beneath the seat like a beating heart. It's dark on the backroads, no streetlights, the pinelands nothing more than indications of mass on either side.

When Sheeler pulls over, Tom pulls over behind him, not bothering to turn off his headlights. He thinks Sheeler must be onto him, but Sheeler is just taking a piss. He walks unsteadily to the side of the pinelands and unzips his pants. By the time he turns to look at the headlights of the truck behind him, Tom is bracing the rifle on the door, the way he did the night he shot the ranger outside Gettysburg. Sheeler's pale white face, his white hands, his tattooed forearms. He's like a specter. Like something that embodies everything Tom tried to leave behind: South Jersey and its rotten egg stench.

He'd known he was going to, but it still surprises him when he pulls the trigger.

A Brief but Flaring and Glorious Life

Just coming down from the high of getting his ass handed to him in a fight that lasted almost half an hour, Mackey looked in the rearview mirror to see how bad the damage was. It was not good. You should see the other guy. The other guy had almost fifty pounds and six inches on him, but he'd left the parking lot behind the old industrial park with a mouthful of blood from an uppercut to the jaw. With Mackey, the damage was more general. His cheekbone, his temples, a bunch of welts. The guy wore a class ring that had left the imprint of a devil mascot on his cheek. Gracie was going to be pissed. His face already had so much scar tissue it could have been a mask covering what used to be the face of a pretty sweet guy. Back when he was innocent.

The fact that he'd been able to pick himself up after ceding the fight was a feat all its own. There wasn't always the possibility of calling a fight. Sometimes he woke up in the ER two towns over with brain injuries. Broken ribs. Once a broken arm thanks to a crowbar some mean fucker had taken to him. And then there were the times he'd actually won. He tried to stop before going too far, but that killer instinct was awakened in him pretty easy, and once it was there, forget about it. He'd come back to himself while pounding some poor fuck's head into the pavement, one millimeter away from killing someone. No one pressed charges because they were all out there to fuck each other up. It was what they did, of a Saturday night. What else was there to do? They were far from anything that could be considered a city, in the bright blue wilderness of East Bumfuck, New Hampshire.

Maybe he was getting a little old for it.

His head ached and his ears rang and all he wanted to do was have Gracie nestle him between her big titties. He wasn't sure he'd be up to the act itself, but some fooling around was most definitely in order. A second, smaller spike of adrenaline and then off to lala land. To sleep perchance to dream. Mackey liked his dreams, even when, maybe especially when, they got weird as hell. A messy hodgepodge of his dumb life. His time in Afghanistan, his fighting life, his work life—what a shitshow that was; he worked at the local transfer station—and women, all kinds of women. Sometimes Gracie herself made an appearance in his dreams. She was the sexiest woman he knew, but that didn't stop the others from crowding into his dreams, celebrities of course, but mainly women wrestlers, the kind with bulging biceps and thighs that could squeeze the life out of him. Torrie Wilson, Lita, Chyna. Sometimes all he wanted to do was go to sleep and live in that world for as long as he could.

He was half-hard when he pulled down the dirt road that was supposed to be paved one of these days, flanked by deep dark New Hampshire forest and a couple trailers, his and Gracie's at the end, but he went full soft when he saw the little white Hyundai parked in what passed as a driveway but was really just a flat patch of dirt he'd covered with little rocks. The Korean provenance of the car pissed him off, but it was what the car carried to his home that really irked him. Gracie's friend Tina, a grown ass woman with the body of a ten-year-old girl. Flat, petite. Her face, even though they were all only in their thirties, already had the slack leather expression of an old woman. She was a walking contradiction, and also his enemy. She was always badmouthing him when he wasn't around, trying to convince Gracie to leave him. He'd thought, more than a few times, about getting Tina by herself and offing her. Not seriously, but not unseriously either.

He got out of the car, straightened his shirt and brushed off his pants, but there was nothing he could do about his face. His ears rang and the shiners were rising to the surface of his skin, and now that he'd stopped driving he could see out of only one eye, the other bruised shut.

The ladies sat at the kitchen table listening to Van Halen, *Diver Down*. A good album, though maybe a little too typical for his taste. "Where Have All the Good Times Gone" transitioned to "Hang Em High." The way they looked at him… he felt ashamed, and feeling ashamed made him angry, and feeling angry made him feel angry at himself for feeling angry. He tried to keep it all inside but felt it all tea-kettling behind his scarred and battered face.

"We need to talk, Mackey," Gracie said. She looked up at him like a dog that knows it's done something it shouldn't have. Gracie, he thought. Gracie, Gracie, Gracie. With her big titties hidden in a big black Pantera t-shirt. His Pantera t-shirt. He flashed back to the week before when she'd dolled up in a red dress for him. Plenty of cleavage. They'd gone out to eat at the Bonefish Grill near Concord. They'd had drinks, talked about their future, fucked like crazy, fallen asleep like children of Eden or something. She was always trying to get him to go to church, and they'd gone together that next day. She'd looked almost as sexy in her church clothes as she had in her going-out clothes, and they'd fucked that day, too. It had been like the beginning again. True, the week following had gotten rough, what with work and her nagging at him. He'd had to let off steam a couple times, but a couple nights they'd watched TV together. What did she want, a perfect man? It ain't me, Babe.

"We can talk without her around." He gestured to Tina, who sat real close to Gracie, her hand on the phone sitting there on the kitchen table. Ready to call the cops if things went south. She screwed up her rat face at him.

"She's here to support me. I'm leaving."

"It don't look like you're leaving."

He had a talent for saying the exact wrong thing. Gracie got up, walked toward the bedroom. She was wearing loose gray sweatpants and slippers, but she pulled an already-packed bag out of the bedroom. So, it was actually happening. She was actually leaving him. He felt like slamming the little bitch's face into the kitchen table. Tina, not Gracie. Felt like cutting her head off and watching blood spume up from the stump of her neck. It was his fault, all of it, he knew it was, but Tina, Tina was the cause of it all. She held the phone headset as if it were a trigger, ready to pull it. Didn't she realize it would be too late if she tried? That he'd stop her one way or the other before she could call anyone? He imagined how satisfying the crunch of her nose beneath his fist would feel.

He was still picturing it when the door of the trailer closed and he listened to the engine of the Hyundai start up and drive away.

In the morning, he seemed to be floating, his head in thick cotton batting that was almost visible. He puked up everything he ate and he had a headache, couldn't even jerk off without feeling like his head was going to explode, and he wondered if this was it, was he going to die like this? Alone? He smelled Gracie on the pillow and, ashamed, he clutched it to himself and cried. Then he took a shower.

He sat at the kitchen table picturing all kinds of things, none of them good. He'd been with Gracie almost ten years.

Ups and downs. When his mother died, she'd comforted him. When he lost his job, she stuck with him until he found a new one. The transfer station, where he was the lowest of the low. For now. She was waiting for him to get down on his knee and ask her to be his wife, but something always stopped him. Maybe he'd known they were no good for each other. He'd never hit her, but he'd grabbed her arm hard enough to leave a bruise. She yelled at him, sometimes threw things. They got into a state sometimes. Maybe it was better to be apart. For both of them. He missed laying his head on her big titties. The pillow of them. She was the only one had ever seen him cry.

Tina lived near the part of town with strip malls and grocery stores, above a laundromat. Inside the apartment it always smelled like dryer. They'd gone there maybe three times, when Tina had a man, trying to do the couples thing. Played cards, smoked, drank. The other guy had been smaller than him, a college graduate, someone who was clearly only temporary. No one could take Tina for long. He pictured punching her in the leather face over and over again, the stunned look in her old lady eyes.

The only real hope he had was to calm down and let things ride. If he could get himself under control he had a chance to get Gracie back. He parked beside the white Hyundai, looked up at the windows of Tina's apartment. Had a sudden vivid picture of the two of them going down on each other. Big and little. The weird symmetry of it like a yin-yang symbol. Something pulsed behind his eyeballs. A pain different than the pain after most fights.

He got out and took the tire iron from his trunk. He felt the way he did when he was in the middle of a fistfight, that mix of perfect control and no control at all. Another part of him had taken over. It was an evil, angry part of him, but it was pure, and if he could find a way to live inside that part of himself all the time he would have. It would be a brief but flaring and glorious life.

The connection of the tire iron with the headlight of the Hyundai was perfection, like dancing or art. He followed through, heard the smashing, felt the reverberations in his arms, forgot all about the pain in his head, was there but not really there at the same time. Lived in that moment for as long as he could.

Acknowledgments

Gratefully acknowledged are the following publications, where stories appeared in earlier versions:

"Charlie's," "A Crash on the Highway," "The Day After Easter," and "Always and Utter Bullshit": *Bull Fiction*

"Savor Life": *Bang!* (Head Shot Press)

"The Bar Built in an Old Sheet Metal Factory": *The Rye Whiskey Review*

"Everything Rises": *Shotgun Honey*

"Idiotic American Boys": *Mystery Tribune Online*

"It Never Snows in Vietnam": *Poverty House*

"Artifacts of the Civil War": *Schuylkill Valley Review*

"The Resurrection Project": *Hidden Peaks Press*

"Butch": *Syntax*

"San Juan": *Punk Noir*

"Love as an Act of Revenge": *I Feel Just Like a Dogwood Tree* (Cowboy Jamboree Press). The story was inspired by the concept album *Juarez* by Terry Allen.

"Bodies in Bags": *Cowboy Jamboree*

"The Body in Lake Montebello": *Revolution John*

"A Brief but Flaring and Glorious Life": *Bristol Noir*

Massive thanks to Evangeline Gallagher for being an amazing daughter and illustrating *two* book covers.

Massive thanks to Alexander Gallagher just for being so freakin' cool and kind.

Massive thanks to Kris Messer for being the one.

Massive thank to my mother, Maureen Gallagher, and brother, Chris.

Thanks to mentors: Andre Dubus III, Ann Green, J.C. Hallman, Jo Parker, April Lindner, Tom Coyne.

Thanks to Karry Albert Gallagher.

Thanks to fellow writers: Anne Vukicevich, Melanie Kuchma, Ted Fristrom, Sam Kimball, Kim Jensen, Dave Truscello, Jeff Esterholm, Toby LeBlanc, Benjamin Drevlow, Libby Cudmore, and Anna Vangala Jones

Thanks to forever friends: Chris Battles, Paul Baylis, Mark Webster, Ross DeHarportte, and Erin Battles.

Thanks to the inimitable Dr. Ross Tangedal and the talented and patient Brett Hill at Cornerstone Press. Thanks to Nathan Pearson, Jazmyne Johnson, Lillian Kulback, Grady Roesken, Ellie Atkinson, and Asher Shroeder for working on edits.

I wasn't sure I would get the chance to publish even one book, so publishing this second book is a thrill for me.

JAMEY GALLAGHER is the author of *American Animism* (Cornerstone Press 2024). His stories have been published in more than seventy venues, including *Punk Noir Magazine, Shotgun Honey, Pembroke Magazine, Bull Fiction,* and *LIT Magazine.* He lives in Baltimore and teaches at the Community College of Baltimore County.

www.ingramcontent.com/pod-product-compliance
Lightning Source LLC
LaVergne TN
LVHW040050080526
838202LV00045B/3570